EMPRESS IN DANGER

EMPRESS IN DANGER

EMPRESS IN DISGUISE BOOK 3

ZOEY GONG

AMANDA ROBERTS

Red Empress Publishing
www.RedEmpressPublishing.com

Copyright © Zoey Gong
www.ZoeyGong.com

Copyright © Amanda Roberts
www.AmandaRobertsWrites.com

Cover by Cherith Vaughan
CoversbyCherith.com

ALSO BY ZOEY GONG

Contemporary Romance

The New Year Boyfriend

The Animal Companions Series

A Girl and Her Elephant

A Girl and Her Panda

A Girl and Her Tiger

Empress in Disguise Trilogy

Empress in Disguise

Empress in Hiding

Empress in Danger

ALSO BY AMANDA ROBERTS

<u>Fiction Novels</u>

Threads of Silk

The Man in the Dragon Mask

<u>The Qing Dynasty Mysteries</u>

Murder in the Forbidden City

Murder in the British Quarter

Murder at the Peking Opera

<u>The Touching Time Series</u>

The Child's Curse

The Emperor's Seal

The Empress's Dagger

The Slave's Necklace

<u>Empress in Disguise Trilogy</u>

Empress in Disguise

Empress in Hiding

Empress in Danger

<u>Nonfiction</u>

The Crazy Dumplings Cookbook

Crazy Dumplings II: Even Dumplinger

1

The sweet scent of the chrysanthemums I just planted fills my nose. I look around, satisfied with my work planting a dozen chrysanthemum plants in different colors in a flowerbed along one side of the abbey where I have lived and worked for months. I sit on my heels and look around at the thick forest that isolates the abbey from the outside world. A bright ray of sunshine filters through the pine needles, and birds chirp as they jump from branch to branch. It is summer, but here in the mountains, surrounded by trees, it is a cool and comfortable place.

I stand up, dust off my knees, and carry my basket of gardening supplies to a small work shed. I rinse my hands with water from a nearby water pump and drink the cool, fresh water. From a nearby building, a gong is struck, the sound reverberating across the abbey. Slowly, dozens of women dressed the same way I am, in simple orange robes, cross the courtyard toward the main temple. Some of the women have shaved heads. Some of the women, though, like me, have their long hair wound upon their heads and covered with orange fabric. The women who live here are not forced to shave their heads, as it is a deeply personal act, but most do eventually. I do not think I will take such a step anytime soon.

At a giant, iron brazier, I stop and light a joss stick, placing it in the thick ash of the thousands of joss sticks before it so that it stands upright, the pleasing smoke ascending to the heavens. I then climb the stairs of the temple and find an empty spot to perform a kowtow to the eight-foot-tall statue of Guanyin, the goddess of mercy, the woman who protects and blesses us.

I kowtow seven times, and then seven more times, each time uttering a traditional prayer that speaks of Guanyin's goodness and asks for her mercy. By the time I am finished, my head is spinning. I sit on my heels for a moment and take a breath. I wait for my sisters, my fellow nuns, to leave so that I may speak to Guanyin alone, in my own words, as I do every day.

"Guanyin, goddess of mercy," I say, my eyes closed and my hands folded before me. "You have been kind to me, of that I am certain. More than once, I should have died. I deserved to die. I did not know why I lived, what my purpose was. But I believe all my trials sent me here to you.

"I am not deserving, but I will once again plead upon your mercy. Please, please, please, help me find my family. They are good people, loving people, and I know they worry about me. I only wish to let them know that I am safe. I cannot bear the thought that they may think I am dead, that the emperor killed me for my sins against him.

"If you find it in your heart to grant me this wish, I will never again ask for anything. I will worship you for all of my days."

I kowtow seven more times, and then I try to stand. I

perform this ritual three times a day and have done so for months. Still, as I push myself to my feet, my knees scream in pain and I hobble across the room like an old woman. There are some sisters, many much older than I am, who pray more often, and for longer periods of time, but they do not limp as I do when they stand. I suppose I shall have to wait a very long time before my body becomes as strong as theirs.

I light another joss stick and place it in a trough that runs the length of the three-foot-high dais where Guanyin reclines, leaning on her hand on one side, her other arm propped up on her bent knee. She looks down at me kindly, as though asking me to sit awhile and tell her my problems. And I have, many times. She is the only person I trust with my complete story.

Tao Fashi, the senior teacher here and head of the abbey, has been very patient with me. I have told her several parts of my story, but not all of it. There are some parts that I am ashamed to speak of. And then there are parts that I still feel could be too dangerous to speak aloud. She does not know who I really am. She knows my name, but not the significance of it. It is Manchu tradition for people to change their name at significant points in their lives. Tao Fashi knows that I was known as Lihua when I was the empress, and she knows that I now use the name Daiyu. But she does not know that Daiyu is my real name, the name given to me by my parents. A name I had to abandon when I agreed to take the place of a Manchu girl who did not want to become the emperor's consort. Here, at the Temple of Grief, I hope the emperor has forgotten me. If that is true, then perhaps, one day, I will be able to tell my story. But until then, I will tell no one. I fear not only for myself, but anyone who knows the truth. If Tao Fashi knew who I was and did not inform the emperor, she could be punished for taking part in my deception should the emperor learn of it. I do not want anyone to ever suffer for the mistakes I have made.

When I am finished praying, I stand up, dust myself off, and go to one of the buildings in the temple complex that is used as a classroom.

"Daiyu! Come sit by me," a woman named Chan-juan calls out when I enter the room. She is sitting on her heels at a low table that is covered with paper and writing utensils. I sit on a cushion across from her. She pushes her inkstone toward the middle of the table where I can reach it. I pick up a horsehair brush and wet the bristles, waiting for them to soften.

"Here," Chan-juan says, showing me a piece of paper with a short letter written on it. "Can you read this?"

Since I am the youngest person living at the convent, many of the nuns have taken me under their wings, caring for me, teaching me, giving me shoulders to cry on. Life here has not always been easy. There have been many days I have considered simply walking away. But it is the best place I could be right now. I have nowhere else to go. So, I have made the best of my time here by putting all my effort into learning to read, write, and do basic math. When I was living in the Forbidden City, my eunuch, Jinhai, did his best to teach me, but there were many distractions and responsibilities that used up most of my day, so I did not learn very much in the time I was there. Here at the convent, I seem to have nothing but time.

I scan the letter Chan-juan has given me, and I can easily make sense of most of it. It is a letter to her sister, asking how things are in the family.

I nod. "There are a few characters I don't think I've seen

before," I say, pointing them out. Chan-juan explains them to me, then I get to work copying the letter onto my own paper.

"Your handwriting has steadily improved," Chan-juan says approvingly.

"Yes," I say. "Dongmei and Jiangfei would be proud." My breath shudders and my hand shakes at the thought of the emperor's daughters. My daughters. I miss them so much and worry about what will happen to them without me there to protect them. I have written to them—well, I've had Chan-juan or another woman write to them on my behalf—many times. Weekly, in fact. But I have never received a reply. I hope that they are receiving my letters but have been forbidden to reply to me. But I know that it is far more likely that they have never received a single one. The emperor's mother, the Dowager Empress Fenfeng, probably delights in burning them herself when they are delivered.

Chan-juan reaches across the table and places a hand on my arm. "I know they would be."

I look at her and try to force a reassuring smile, but I cannot. My lips quiver and I feel tears running down my cheeks. I have stopped writing, the ink flowing from the brush onto the paper and creating a large, black circle. I put the brush down until I can control myself.

"I miss them all so much," I say, and Chan-juan nods. I am speaking of Dongmei and Jiangfei, but also of my own family, my parents and sisters. I still have had no contact with them, nor have I tried to. I cannot ask anyone to write such a letter on my behalf without revealing who I am. That is the main reason I have worked so hard to learn to read and write on my own. Someday, I will write to my family, but only when I can write the words myself and then seal them from prying eyes.

"Daiyu! Your doting public has arrived," another nun calls into the room, a playful smile on her face. I sigh and follow her out into the courtyard where three women and two children wait for me. They all bow when they see me.

"May the empress live ten-thousand years!" they say. I walk over to them and ask them to stand.

"I'm not the empress anymore," I say, though I know the words will have no effect on them. Every day, women venture to the temple from around the country to pay their respect to me. I tell them to stop, but that seems to make the people love me more. They return home and speak of my humility to others, who then want to come and meet me for themselves. I wish I could act spoiled and entitled instead. Maybe then they would grow to despise me and stop coming. But I can't do that. I'm entitled to nothing, and I never want anyone to believe that I think I am.

"You will always be our empress, my lady," one of the women says on behalf of the group. "You saved our lives. Saved our country! The emperor cannot erase that, and he can never erase you."

I smile and nod in appreciation as she hands me a basket of kumquats. The other women have bags of rice and beans, and these they give to some of the other nuns who have joined us. The children give us dates and red beans, along with hugs.

Tao Fashi then joins us, and the first woman discreetly hands her a bundle of coins on a red string. Tao Fashi folds her hands together and bows to the woman in thanks. The group then moves to the iron brazier to light joss sticks before going to pray inside the temple. The other nuns then take the food items to the kitchen.

I do wish the people would stop coming to me. Stop speaking about me and sharing my story. The emperor has banished me, erased me from the official record. I am afraid that should he still hear about me, especially the people speaking well of me, he will become even more angry and order my death. But I am glad that the gifts people bring benefit the whole temple, not just me. I have kept nothing for myself, but donate everything I receive to the temple.

"Your grief sits upon your shoulders like a great weight," Tao Fashi says, calling me back to the present.

"Greif, regret..." I shrug my shoulders. "A great many things."

She nods and hands me an empty basket. "Why don't you go and gather mushrooms. A walk in the woods is restorative to the soul."

I take the basket and bow to my teacher. I know the real reason she is sending me out of the temple is so that I do not have to face the women and children who have come to see me again. I can slip away until they are gone.

I go through the wide gate and down the many steps, turning into the pinewood forest about halfway down the staircase. Pine needles and cones crunch under my steps, no matter how delicately I walk. I reach up and tug at the orange cloth around my head. It pulls free easily, and my hair tumbles down around my shoulders. I run my fingers through it, lamenting how coarse and tangly it has become. Of course, when I was growing up, my hair was in even worse condition. But living in the palace, Suyin would brush my hair every morning and evening with a tortoise-shell comb dipped in scented oil to make my hair smooth and soft. I think having my hair bound all the time is not helping it. Like me, my hair needs to breathe and feel the sunlight. I pull my hair around my shoulder and pick at a knot that has formed.

I have not walked very far when I feel...uneasy. As if I

am not alone. I turn around, expecting to see someone. Perhaps a nun who has come to walk with me or a curious child who has followed me. But I see no one.

I try to shake the feeling off as I continue walking toward a rotting fallen tree where mushrooms always seem to sprout. This is not the first time I have felt the need to look over my shoulder. Even though the emperor banished me, I still fear his wrath. What if he sends someone to kill me? Or the dowager empress does? I know that she was behind the deaths of Lady An and Empress Caihong. I could never prove it, of course, but the fact that I know could make me a threat to her. Or she could simply wish me dead because she hates me. These thoughts make me look over my shoulder again, but I still see no one.

I climb over the dead tree and crouch down on the other side to collect the mushrooms. They grow in bunches, like white fans, and are one of my favorite kinds of mushrooms. Though, I love all mushrooms and can eat them raw. Except wood ear mushrooms. I can hardly abide to look at them, much less eat them. The brown, floppy, chewy texture is enough to turn my stomach—

I freeze when I hear the sound of pine needles crunching, as if under a footstep. A chill runs down my spine and my arms break into goose flesh. My heart races and I can hardly hear anything over the sound of blood thumping in my ears. I slowly sit up and peek over the top of the fallen tree.

Still, I see nothing. But that brings me no comfort and only makes me more afraid. Whoever is out there is deliberately hiding from me. I crouch back down and hold my basket tight, though I will hardly be able to defend myself with a mere basket. I look around for a solid tree branch or anything I might be able to brandish as a weapon, but I can find nothing of use.

I hear the crunching again, closer this time. I cover my mouth with my hand to keep from crying out loud, rocking back and forth on my knees. If I can't defend myself, then I must hide. My pursuer probably saw me climb over the log, so I cannot stay here. There are no other places of cover within crawling distance, though. I will have to dart through the trees in a confusing manner. Hopefully, I can lose him that way and make it back to the temple. I will be safe there. No one would dare attempt to shed blood under the watchful eye of the goddess.

I hear a step, and another, and another. Steady, small steps growing closer. I cannot wait. I jump to my feet and dart ahead, my mushrooms spilling from my basket.

But I don't get far.

I scream as I nearly run into a large buck. He seems startled as well, rearing up on his back legs and letting out a strangled sort of growl. I stumble back, falling on my rear as he lands on his feet, the ground tremoring slightly under his weight. He then darts away, practically bouncing through the trees as he escapes my view.

I let out a heavy sigh of relief. The footsteps had been nothing more than a deer. I should have known that. We are rather secluded out here, and wildlife is plentiful. I feel like an idiot as I stand and brush myself off. I turn around to go back to the log and collect the mushrooms I dropped, but I scream again when I see a person standing just on the other side of the log.

"My lady!" Suyin bows, bending down on her knees. "I didn't mean to startle you."

It takes a moment for my breath to come back to me and my heart to stop racing enough for me to speak.

"Su— Suyin?" I can hardly believe what I am seeing. For a fleeting moment, I wonder if she is a ghost.

"Yes," she says, standing, her hands folded tightly in front of her. "It's me."

I blink a few times. "What...what are you doing here?"

She climbs over the log. "I came to be with you, my lady."

"What? Why?"

"I...I missed you," she says sheepishly.

I shake my head, my mouth still agape. Questions run through my head, all crashing together. Why is she here? *How* is she here? Why was she hiding? Should I send her away? Has something terrible happened?

Suyin nervously chews on her lower lip, waiting for my response. But I cannot speak. Above all the questions, all the doubts, is such a sense of relief at seeing my maid, my friend, I can only cry. I drop my basket and quickly walk to Suyin, grabbing her and pulling her into my arms. I burst into tears as she hugs me back. I did not realize just how lonely I had been until this moment.

There is so much to say, so much I need to ask, but all that can wait. For now, I hold my friend in my arms and cry until there are no tears left.

2

———

I wipe the tears from my cheeks. "What are you doing here?"

"I...I couldn't stay there," she says, somewhat shamefaced.

"Why? What's happened? The emperor..." I can't bring myself to ask the question most on my mind.

"He's alive...barely," she says. "The doctors don't know how he has managed to hold on for so long. His wounds have healed somewhat, at least on the outside. But as soon as he heals from one infection, another follows. He is in constant pain. He hasn't left his bed. Prince Honghui has been standing in as the emperor in all but name."

At the mention of Honghui, I have to sit on a nearby log. I have not allowed myself to think of him. At least, I have tried to stop myself from doing so. But late at night, when the only noise is the chirrup of crickets and the hooting of owls, I can think of nothing else.

"What is wrong?" Suyin asks, kneeling by me and taking my hand.

I shake my head. "Nothing. Just...memories..." I can see

the prince's face clearly in my mind. The worry across his brow. The darkness under his eyes from not sleeping. The strain of ruling—a burden that should never have been his —weighing heavily on his shoulders. Even from far away, and even though I have not seen him in so long, I know how he must suffer.

I clear my throat and the memories away as I stand to resume my search for mushrooms. I pull Suyin up to walk next to me, arm in arm, through the woods.

"So, why are you here?" I ask again. "Something must have happened to drive you away."

"It's the dowager empress," she says as we walk together. "She has become intolerable. The emperor has been too ill to choose a new empress. Even if he did, I don't think any of the ladies would have the strength to take her rightful place as head of the harem. Fenfeng rules over all of us, and she never lets us forget it."

"What did she do to you?"

"I was demoted to kitchen maid, scrubbing pots," she says, her nose wrinkling. "And worse. Any disdainful job she could think of, I was ordered to do it."

"I'm sorry," I say. "But why come here? I gave you plenty of money. You could return home."

"My parents would never allow me to desert my post so shamefully. The only honorable way I could leave service would be through marriage. And I don't think Fenfeng was interested in finding me a husband any time soon. And if she did..." She shudders. "I can't imagine who her choice would be. Certainly a butcher or a gravedigger."

I nod. Butchers occupy a strange place in society. They do hard, necessary work. But having to kill and spill blood... The very thought makes me ill. Even if such a man earns an honest wage, to be promised in marriage to a butcher is a great indignity for any woman.

"Your parents are sure to learn of your actions," I say. "When Fenfeng notices you are gone, she will send messengers to them to find you."

"And they will honestly be able to say that they have no idea where I am. Eventually, when Fenfeng has forgotten me, I will tell my parents that I have dedicated myself to Heaven. They will be disappointed, of course, but I will send them the money you gave me. I am sure that the amount will be enough to earn their forgiveness."

"I am glad to have you here," I say. "But it will be up to Tao Fashi whether or not you can stay with us."

"If she does not allow me to stay in the abbey, then I will live here in the woods. I'll not leave you."

I try to smile but cannot without tears forming again. "And what of Jinhai?" I ask. "Has he fared any better?"

"No," she says sadly. "But as a eunuch, he cannot leave the palace. If he were caught, he would immediately be put to death. I stayed as long as I did for him. We were a team. But he eventually insisted I go. No sense us both being miserable, he said."

I come upon a large cluster of mushrooms and bend down to pick them. Suyin helps me. "I wish there was something I could do for him."

"I do not think there is," Suyin says. "Even if Fenfeng were to die, you do not exist. I don't know who would be the head of the harem then. Yanmei, I suppose. She has not been in the harem the longest, but she is the highest-ranking of the emperor's ladies. I suppose she should be serving as the empress now, but Fenfeng will not allow it."

"Poor Yanmei." Yanmei had been a dear friend to me. I

had meant to do her a great honor by promoting her. But I fear I have put her directly in Fenfeng's path instead.

We stand up and I brush my dirty hands on my plain robe. Suyin smirks. "Is that how you dress every day?"

I have to chuckle. Even Suyin, in her servant's robe and after traveling for days, if not weeks, looks more like a lady than I do.

"Well, it is easy to dress myself."

"You won't have to do that anymore," Suyin says. "I can help you."

"No," I say firmly. "There are no servants or masters here. We all serve only the goddess. In a strange way, I feel honored to dress this way. I did not realize how much I missed living a simple life."

Suyin cocks her head curiously. "What do you mean?"

I feel my cheeks go hot at my blunder. Even Suyin never knew the truth of my identity. Even now, she thinks I was raised as the daughter of a military commander and a noblewoman. I was never going to tell her. But now...I suppose I don't have a choice.

I chuckle uneasily and slip my arm through hers. "Come," I say, leading her back to the abbey. "We have much to talk about."

⁓

*A*t the end of my story, Suyin puts her cup down on the low tea table that sits between us and is silent. She opens her mouth to speak, then closes it again. I see several expressions cross her face. Confusion, sadness, and even anger. Her silence unnerves me, and I am oddly relieved that I still did not reveal the full extent of my secrets to her. I did not tell her of my love affair with Prince

Honghui. That is something I think I must take to my grave.

"Please, say something," I beg. I reach across the table to take her hands, but she slides them away, putting them in her lap. Tears fill my eyes, but I do my best to hold them back. I have no right to be hurt by her reaction. I was the one who wronged her, who lied to her all this time.

"You were the empress," she finally says softly. "The empress of China. Wife of the emperor. But you...you are not even Manchu."

"I know," I say.

"I had more right to your position than you did," she says, her voice growing louder, sharper. "And yet I served you! Dressed you, bathed you, cleaned your chamber pot."

"I never wanted any of that!" I say. "I never wanted to be chosen."

"All the greater the insult!" she says in a huff, crossing her arms.

"Suyin, I'm sorry," I say. "But what else could I have done? Tell me."

"You should have never taken Mingxia's offer," she says.

"I know," I say. "But my family was starving. I know you come from a poor family, but your father still had a good position. A reliable income. You never went to bed hungry, did you?"

Her anger softens a little. "No," she admits. "I suppose I can't fault you for wanting to help your family. I've sent almost all of my money home too. My father hasn't left his position yet, but he will. He's bought a house with a bit of farmland around it. He says that once the first harvest comes in, he'll be able to earn enough money to only work for himself."

There is a stabbing pain in my heart and I nod. How I

hope my father also used his money wisely. I wish I had been able to contact him. I would have sent them so much more after I was made empress. Enough that Father wouldn't even need a farm to support him and my sisters. He could just live on the money I sent him and never have to worry for anything.

"I am happy for him," I say. "I never wanted to help myself, only others."

Suyin scrutinizes my face for a moment, as if she is looking for more lies. I don't think she sees any because in this, I am being wholly truthful.

"At least I now know why you were so generous compared to the other ladies. I was grateful, of course, but it seemed so strange to me. For a long time, I didn't send the money to my father or spend an ounce of it. I hid it away, always afraid you were going to change your mind and ask for it back."

"You didn't trust me?" I ask, surprised. Not that I was worthy of trust, but I never thought she suspected me of any deceit.

She shrugs. "I don't know. It was just...a feeling. A feeling that something about you wasn't quite right. You were just so...strange. Especially for a lady."

"You have good instincts," I say. "You were right not to trust me. I *was* lying. I *was* deceiving you, and everyone else. There was no malice in it. It was I who lived in constant fear. But you couldn't have known that, known that my intentions were good."

Suyin gives a small nod and goes quiet again. She picks up her now cold teacup and sips at it. Neither of us says anything for a long time.

"Are you...still angry with me?" I finally dare to ask. I am not sure I want to hear the answer, but the silence gnaws at me.

"No," Suyin says with a defeated sigh. "I wish I were, but I'm not. I am more hurt, I think. Hurt that you never told me the truth. That you never trusted me enough to tell me the truth after all we went through. I guess if I never came here, I would never have known."

I have to nod in agreement. "I wish I'd had enough courage to tell you sooner. You and Jinhai."

"Poor Jinhai," Suyin says, shaking her head. "He'll never know, I suppose."

"Maybe I could write to him," I say.

"You can write?" she asks.

"Not very well," I have to admit. "But the sisters here have been so gracious to me. I've learned a lot since coming here."

"And do they know the truth?" she asks.

I shake my head. "No, not even Tao Fashi. Even here, so far away from the Forbidden City, I am afraid of my secret coming to light. I don't want to put anyone here in danger."

"Well, you should not write to Jinhai," Suyin says. "Anyone could intercept the letter. I think you are right to still be cautious. Even though the emperor banished you, erased you, no one has really forgotten you. If your true identity were discovered, it might anger people."

"Exactly," I say. "Thank you for understanding."

"As it is, the people still love you. They still talk about the empress who saved the empire. The empress who saved them from starvation in the mountains. They leave offerings outside the gate and burn incense."

My heart races and the fear that had been lingering in the back of my mind rushes forward. I almost want to flee, but where would I go?

"Is the emperor very angry about it?" I ask. "I knew that some people remembered me. They come here, to the temple, and give me gifts. I donate everything to Tao Fashi and the abbey. But I had hoped it was only a few people who thought of me. I don't want attention."

She waves her hand dismissively. "The emperor hardly knows what is happening in his room, much less beyond the great red walls. The dowager empress, however, it displeases her greatly. She has the guards remove the offerings daily and run off the petitioners. But they always come back the next day."

I unsuccessfully try to stifle a chuckle. I fear the dowager, greatly, but a small part of me can't help but be amused that my presence still lingers to vex her. Suyin giggles as well.

"Are we...on good terms again?" I ask.

"We will be," she says. "I am still hurt, and a bit overwhelmed by everything you have told me. It will take time for the pain to heal, but I do forgive you."

Tears of relief spring from my eyes and I put my hand to my mouth to keep from crying out loud. "Thank you," I manage to whisper.

Suyin moves to my side of the table and wraps her arms around me. "But don't think for a moment that I'm ever going to clean your chamber pot again."

I bark a laugh. "I think I can live with that."

A gong is struck, signaling that it is time for evening prayers before bed. I stand and pull Suyin up next to me.

"Come," I say. "I must give thanks to the goddess. I have never had so much to be thankful for."

"I never thought you were very religious," Suyin says as we cross the courtyard together.

"I wasn't," I say. "But I can only credit my survival to divine intervention."

"Perhaps the gods still have plans for you yet," she says thoughtfully.

"I hope not," I say. "If I could live the rest of my life here, in peace and safety, I would be content."

3

I am so excited to have my friend with me—my *friend*, not my maid—that I cannot sleep. I give Suyin my bed until Tao Fashi can find a more permanent place for her and I sleep on the floor. Well, Tao Fashi said "permanent," but I am certain she will not let Suyin stay indefinitely if she does not dedicate herself to the goddess.

But now that Suyin is with me, maybe I will find the strength to leave. I have nothing, but Suyin still has some of the money she earned with her. I know how to live frugally, so even a small amount of money could tide us over for quite some time. Perhaps...perhaps we could try to find my family.

The thought of seeing my family again, hugging my sisters, being hugged by my parents, thrills me so much, I wish we could leave right now. But it is the middle of the night, and the moon is high in the sky. I lie on my back for what seems like hours, staring at the rafters above me in the large, shared room where a dozen women sleep. They all breathe evenly, deeply, not least of all Suyin. She always was a heavy sleeper, which was why I was able to sneak out of my room and meet with Prince Honghui.

I am restless, my feet shaking, itching to move. Finally, I can stand it no longer and throw back the cover of my little pallet. I slip quietly to the door. One of the other women must be a light sleeper as she raises her head and looks toward me, though I do not think she can see who it is in the darkness of the room.

"Shh," I whisper. "Go back to sleep." Her head bobs and then rests back on her pillow. I open and close the door quickly so as not to wake anyone else.

The night air is a little chilly, so I wrap my robe tightly around me and shove my hands into my armpits. It only takes a moment for my eyes to adjust to the darkness. The moon is quite bright and not blocked by trees in the wide, open courtyard. I shuffle across the bricked yard, my linen shoes growing wet with dew.

The doors to the temple are always open, so I step inside and try to shake the wet from my feet. There are braziers lit on either side of the room, and tiny, orange dots from smoldering joss sticks seem to float in midair below the statue of the goddess. I am not surprised to see Tao Fashi kowtowing to the goddess even though it is the middle of the night. In my months here, I have found her praying at various times of the day and night. She is truly the most devout person I have ever met.

Tao Fashi sits up, her hands folded in front of her, a slight smile on her face. She bows to the goddess one last time and then looks directly at me, causing me to start a bit. I thought I had been more quiet than that.

"Come," she says, patting the little pillow next to her. "Sit with me."

"I did not mean to disturb you," I say as I cross the room and fold down to my knees on the pillow.

"You did not disturb me," she says kindly. "I was nearly finished."

"You should return to bed," I say. "It is late and you must be tired."

She chuckles. "At my age, the eternal sleep looms large. There is still much for me to do and I cannot waste what little time I still have on this earth sleeping. You are young and need your rest. It is you who should be sleeping."

I shake my head. "I tried but could not."

"The presence of your friend warms your heart."

"Yes. I did not realize how lonely I was, even surrounded by so many kind and generous women. "

"What will you do now?" she asks, surprising me. As a former wife of the emperor, I am supposed to spend the rest of my life here. Even though that is not the life I desire, I did not think that Tao Fashi would approve of any wish to leave.

"What do you mean? I...I am supposed to stay here."

"And how often in your life have you done what you were supposed to do?"

I blush, unsure how to answer. Does Tao Fashi know more about me than I thought? Was she listening as I told Suyin my story?

"The emperor would not have banished you here if you followed the rules," she says with a smirk.

I breathe a little easier knowing she is still in the dark about my past. I want to tell her the truth, long to tell her, but I have yet to find the courage.

"I am torn," I say. "I always seem to be facing monumental decisions. Decisions that will determine the course of the rest of my life."

"There are no monumental decisions," Tao Fashi says.

"Nor are there inconsequential ones. Every choice you make changes the path of your life. Will you have eggs or baozi for breakfast?"

I shrug. "Does it matter?"

"What if the eggs are rotten and you sicken and die?"

"Oh. I see what you mean." I pause before continuing. "I think I could stay here, try to live a life of peace and quiet. It would not be a bad life. I would be safe here."

She nods. "Many of the women here are content, if not happy."

"Exactly. But equally do I wonder if Suyin's arrival means I should leave. She would come with me, of course, so I would not be alone. Merely having a companion could give me the strength to do what I really want to do—find my family."

For a moment, surprise flashes across Tao Fashi's face. She knows my official history—Empress Lihua's history. The history that says I was raised as the only daughter of a general and high-born lady. This is the first time I have given her any indication that my past is not what she thinks. But her surprise is so fleeting, I have to believe that—like Suyin—Tao Fashi has long suspected that I might not be who I have claimed to be.

"Is your desire to leave truly equal with the desire to stay?" she asks me, and I do not hesitate to answer.

"No. If I were truly free to choose, I would choose my family."

She nodded. "Then I think you have your answer."

My heart sings for a moment. Has Tao Fashi, a woman everyone listens to and respects, given me her permission to leave this place? The feeling of elation lasts only a moment before I am pulled back to reality.

"But it cannot be that simple. If the emperor were to

find out, he would be furious. His mercy would surely be spent. He would want me to be put to death if he ever found me."

"What scares you more," Tao Fashi asks, "to never see your family again, or death for looking for them."

Tears well up in my eyes. I know the answer. My life has been in danger from the moment I accepted Mingxia's money. I do not fear death. Still, part of me is afraid to admit the truth. I guess I have lived behind a shield of lies for so long that the truth frightens me more than an executioner's ax.

"But what about you?" I ask. "If the emperor thinks you let me leave this place or let me escape, he could turn his wrath toward you instead."

Tao Fashi laughs. "I may be old, but I'm not as frail as I look."

"I didn't mean—"

She reaches over and squeezes my shoulder. "You take on far too many of other people's burdens. It shows in the dark parts of your eyes. Such weight you carry! Let them go, Daiyu."

I sigh and can almost feel heavy stones tumbling from my shoulders to the floor. It is a relief, but also do I feel weak. As if I do not know how to stand if I am not carrying my worries with me.

Tao Fashi stands and pulls me up next to her. "Go to bed. Have a rest, and tomorrow the way forward will be more clear to you."

I hug Tao Fashi for a long moment. "Thank you."

She nods and squeezes my shoulders before gently pushing me away. "Go."

As I walk back across the courtyard, I feel so happy, it is a feeling I hardly recognize. I will speak to Suyin as soon as she wakes. She will certainly not want to stay here. It will be hard for me to leave this beautiful and peaceful place, but the thought of finding my family fills me with excitement. I have no idea how I will find them, but I have to at least try.

I open the door to the sleeping quarters and have to blink twice when I see a person standing next to my bed. I think it must be one of the other nuns who has woken early. But as my eyes adjust, I realize that the person is not one of my sisters.

A man dressed all in black, including the lower part of his face, looks at me. When he sees me, his eyes go large as if he has seen a ghost. He looks down at my bed, and then back at me. I look at my bed and see the lump under my blanket that is Suyin.

I then see the knife in the man's hand. The knife dripping black in the darkness. A scream pierces my ears as a pain washes over my body like a tidal wave. The world spins, and I am drowning.

The man who seemed frozen a moment ago stumbles back. I then realize that he hears the scream as well—the scream that is coming from me. I hear a commotion as a brazier is lit and the other sleeping women are startled from sleep.

Suyin does not stir. My scream dies away as I run out of breath and fall to my knees. Screams and shouts fill the room as I crawl toward the bed, my whole body shaking. The man turns and jumps from an open window. There is panic as the women try to make sense of what has happened. Some rush out of the room as if to catch the man. Some women huddle together in fear. But I can only see the lump in my bed that has not moved despite the commotion around it.

I pull the gray blanket back. There, lying on her side,

eyes closed, is Suyin. For a moment, I wonder if I had been dreaming. That the vision of the man had been merely a nightmare. Then I see the dark red stain growing across the thin mattress. I shake Suyin's shoulder. I whisper her name. I tug her onto her back and see the thin slash across her throat. There are gasps from behind me. Someone screams. Someone faints. But I cannot take my eyes off my friend.

She looks as though she is still merely sleeping. Her eyes closed, her mouth slightly parted. I shake her again, hoping that the gash was not deep enough to kill her. She is simply sleeping soundly as she always has. But she doesn't respond.

I shake her again, harder. "Suyin!" I say, my voice stronger. She doesn't move, and the red blood rushes out from the wound at her neck.

"Daiyu," one of the sisters behind me whispers. I feel her hand on my shoulder, and it is then that I accept that this is no dream. Not a nightmare. Suyin, my dear friend, my only friend, is dead.

I groan as I slide my right arm under her head. I wrap my other arm around her chest and hug her tightly. I rock her as I cry into her chest, her warm blood coating us both. I beg the goddess to save her. To take me instead. I know it is too late, but I pray anyway.

Oh, Suyin... My dear Suyin...

4
____

"The dowager did this," I say to Tao Fashi, standing before Suyin's grave. The rest of the sisters have all left us, one by one slinking away back to the abbey. They only attended the funeral out of respect, but none of them knew Suyin. They barely know me. Of course, they all regret the loss of a young life, but none of them mourn her. In all the world, I am the only person alive who does. No one else who knew her knows she is dead. I will have to write to her parents. But what exactly will I tell them? They will want to know what happened to their daughter. I cannot tell them the truth. How could I? If I tell them she was murdered, they will want to know by whom.

I am certain the dowager empress, Fenfeng, is the person who sent the assassin, but I cannot prove it. The assassin escaped into the night. He will never be found. When the empress finds out that he failed to kill me, she will want this head on a pike.

No, the assassin will never be found. Fenfeng will never be held responsible. And Suyin's spirit will forever wander this place as a vengeful ghost. Tao Fashi places a bowl of rice and a plate of oranges before Suyin's grave, offerings to at least prevent the spirit from going hungry.

"Why would Fenfeng want to kill your maid?" she asks, not looking at me. Her face is pale and tired. Lines crease the sides of her mouth and bags are under her eyes. She seems to have aged significantly since Suyin's death only a couple of days ago. It is not from grief, but from the stress and strain Suyin's death has brought to her once peaceful home. The women are all afraid. If a killer could slip in silently among them, no one is safe.

"She didn't," I say. "She sent him to kill me. Suyin was sleeping on my bed. He meant to kill me."

Tao Fashi's jaw tightens as she considers this. "Then he must have been watching you for a few days at least, watching us, if he knew which bed was yours."

I think back to the few, tense moments in the woods before Suyin had made herself known to me. I had been certain that I was not alone. I initially thought Suyin had been the reason for that feeling. But now...now I am not so certain.

"Tao Fashi!" a nun calls out. Tao Fashi gives the woman a small nod.

"I must go. I have duties to attend to. Will you come inside? It may not be safe out here."

I look around the pine forest and hear only birds chirping in the trees. The burial ground is north of the abbey, which I can see on the hill behind us.

"I'll be fine," I say. "I'd like a moment alone with my friend."

Tao Fashi nods and goes with the nun back to the abbey. Once she is gone, I feel completely alone. I do not believe the assassin is nearby, seeking another opportunity to finish this task. Nor do I feel Suyin's spirit hanging around. Is she at peace? Has her spirit already found its way to the hall of her ancestors? I doubt it. How could her soul ever find rest after being murdered so senselessly?

No, she is not at rest. It is more likely that her spirit does not think me worthy of her presence, even to torment me. As my maid, she fulfilled her duty—she served me until the end. And I was not worthy. She will stand by my side no longer.

"I am so sorry," I say, even though I am sure no one is listening. "I will tell your parents. I do not know what I will say, but I will not let them worry over the fate of their daughter. I will send them the money you saved. They will be taken care of." Among Suyin's things, I found her purse. Inside was no small amount. If I took it for myself and lived thriftily, I could probably live off it for the rest of my life. But I will not keep it. It is not mine to take. Somehow, I will make sure it reaches her family.

The sound of galloping horse hooves immediately sets my heart racing. I duck down behind Suyin's grave mound, and it takes me a moment to realize I don't have a reason to be afraid. An assassin wouldn't come riding up to the front gate, plain for all to see.

Still, I am cautious as I creep down toward the road leading to the abbey. I stay low and move from tree to tree, keeping myself as hidden as possible. I see the rider as he reaches the carved stairs leading up to the abbey. It is clear from his armor and helmet that he is an imperial guard. He dismounts and rushes up the stairs in a great hurry, his long ride from the Forbidden City slowing him not at all.

I crouch down in the brush, not sure I want to hear what the guard has come to tell us. In my many months here, we have never received official news from the Forbidden City. Occasionally, some of the nuns have received letters from friends and former servants still living within the great red walls. But not a single letter, missive, or order has arrived from the emperor or on his behalf. Truly, it feels as though the women sentenced to spend the rest of their lives in the Temple of Grief have been forgotten.

Whatever message this imperial guard has brought us must be of great importance. My first thought, naturally, is that the emperor is dead. He had been so grievously injured and seemed to be in such pain when I last saw him. I cover my mouth as I feel sick at the thought. But Suyin said that the emperor had recovered somewhat. And he had been injured months ago. If he were going to die, surely he would have already.

But if not to announce the death of the emperor, why has the messenger come? To announce the death of the dowager empress? No, I think not. We would be informed, certainly, but by an urgent imperial guard? I doubt it.

I then wonder if the empress has somehow learned that her assassin failed. While she will certainly learn of my current state of living soon enough, I do not think she would know of it just yet. Still, I wonder for a moment if it would be better if I remain hidden. Am I being paranoid to wonder if the messenger is here for me specifically?

For another moment, I crouch, sit, and wait until my curiosity gets the better of me and I decide I need to find out whatever it is the messenger has come all this way to say.

I slip silently up the stairs to find most of the nuns gathered in the courtyard. I don't see the messenger anywhere. The nuns share worried whispers with one another about what the messenger's arrival could mean for us.

"Where has he gone?" I ask one of the women who hardly seems to register my presence.

"To speak privately to Tao Fashi," she says, nodding toward the main temple. Her voice is tight and anxious, but her words bring me some relief to know that I am not the man's reason for visiting. Only a moment later, the messenger and Tao Fashi emerge from the temple, speaking low, their heads close together. Tao Fashi's face is grave. She gives a heavy sigh and looks around the courtyard at the gathered women. I try to blend into the crowd and remain unseen, but Tao Fashi's piercing gaze finds me. Her eyes linger on mine for a long moment before she addresses us all.

"My dear sisters," she says, her voice loud and clear but masking pain. "I regret to inform you that Guozhi, our great emperor, is dead."

5

Just as we had after the death of Empress Caihong, everyone in the empire mourned the death of the emperor. We dressed in all white, even covering our long hair with white scarves, and kneeled in the courtyard from dawn until dark. We cried and wailed and kowtowed. Tao Fashi took the lead in singing songs of prayer and mourning, but whenever her voice gave out, one of the other senior sisters would take her place.

The sun was bright and hot and shone down on us for more than twelve hours each day. Our skin burned and our lips cracked, and some of the women passed out from the strain of it all. Still, we kept up the practice for two weeks, as was custom.

For my part, it did not feel as though the mourning had lasted long enough. I do not know if he was a great emperor, or even a good one. I had so doubted his decisions that I openly defied him, even risking my life to do so. But he was a good man. A man who always believed that he was doing the right thing. A man who had been kind to me. A man who had shown me great mercy when I did not deserve it.

He had made me an empress.

But the emperor had died without a son, which had always been one of his greatest fears. I dared not ask who the emperor's successor was, but word reached my ears anyway. Prince Honghui was now the emperor.

I tried not to think about this fact while mourning Emperor Guozhi. It wasn't right for me to do so. Still, as the long, hot days dragged on, it was often only thoughts of Honghui that gave me the strength to endure.

Another emperor had never died in my lifetime, so I had no idea how people in Peking were mourning the loss of one emperor and celebrating the rise of another one at the same time. Still, I imagined Honghui dressed in the sumptuous yellow silk dragon robe of the emperor. His hair washed, oiled, and plaited long down his back. The red-fringed hat upon his head. His face freshly shaven. How handsome, how regal, he must look, sitting upon the dragon throne.

But also, how lonely. His mother had died when he was but a child, as had his father. Guozhi was his only family. He was not yet married, and had no children. My heart ached for him. I wished I could be there by his side, but such a thing was impossible. I was banished here, to the Temple of Grief, and here was where I was to spend the rest of my days. Even if I had not been banished to this place previously, I suppose I would be now. Many of the women who lived here now were widowed consorts of previous emperors. I wondered briefly, happily, if that meant that I would soon see my friend Yanmei again. Dear, kind Yanmei. I had not heard from her since my banishment. I'm sure she was forbidden from writing to me. But what a joy it would be to see her again.

It was these thoughts of old friends, old lovers, that sustained me during the long days and hours of mourning for Emperor Guozhi. I wondered if his death meant that my life was now effectively over as well. There was now no chance of me being summoned back to the Forbidden City. And since Suyin had died, I did not know if I had the courage to ever leave the abbey on my own.

I looked around at my sisters, most well more than twice my age, gray-haired, wrinkled, almost all without children. Was this the future I had to look forward to? But if so, why did the dowager empress send someone to kill me? How could I possibly pose a threat to her now? I was literally no one, my name completely erased from palace records.

True, I did know, or at least believed, that she had also been behind the attempt on Empress Caihong's life. But I could never prove it. Nor did I even want to. The assassination attempt had failed. Caihong had died in childbirth, as far too many women do, to the blame of no one. Of course, what the dowager empress had done was a wicked, evil thing to do, but exposing her now would bring me no peace. I only wanted to erase Fenfeng from my mind completely. Could she not do the same? Forget me as her son had done?

As the sun sets on our fourteenth day of mourning, almost all of the women walk achily to the bathhouse, many leaning on one another for support. Some are so weak they have to be carried away. My knees hurt so greatly, the pain it causes when I try to move does not seem worth the effort. I move, inch by belabored inch, from kneeling to sitting. I am in no rush. Where would I go? I had kneeled for two weeks, what was a few hours more?

"Fourteen days of meditation, yet still your mind seems

troubled," Tao Fashi says as she approaches me. She has dragged a small stool along with her to sit upon. At her age, her knees must be far more sore than mine. I feel a twinge of guilt that I should complain of aches and pains when I am still so young. I attempt to complete my transition to a sitting position more quickly and instantly regret it, crying out in pain as my eyes water.

"Do not rush!" Tao Fashi says, gripping my arm to keep me from toppling over.

I let out an annoyed chuckle. "Ah! How is it that you are the one helping me?" I instantly regret my words, fearing that Tao Fashi might think my words an insult, but she only laughs.

"A woman grows only stronger with age," she says. For some reason, her words remind me of my mother. After all she had been through, so many births, at least one devastating miscarriage, illness, starvation, and yet she endured, year after year. I wonder where she was now and if she ever found the rest she so rightly deserved.

"What is troubling you?" Tao Fashi asks again once we are both somewhat comfortable.

"No one thing," I say. "I suppose I am just caught between wondering what will happen next or thinking that nothing will come next. The emperor is gone and I am here." I give a small shrug. "What else is there for me?"

Tao Fashi nods knowingly. "For so long, it was emperor Guozhi who was in complete control of your life. Without him, I suppose you feel like a ship, rudderless. Captainless. Drifting."

"I suppose so," I say. "Even though I had not seen him for months before his death, even though he had banished me, erased me, my life was his to command. Now that he is gone, does that mean my life is over? Or is my future now wide open?"

Tao Fashi tutted her tongue and shook her head with a bit of an annoyed chuckle. "You are far too young to be wary about such things. You have no idea what changes in your life could be waiting for you when the sun rises tomorrow."

"I doubt my life will change that much in a day," I say.

"Perhaps," Tao Fashi says. "But Emperor Guozhi's widowed consorts will be arriving soon, before the week is out. There will certainly be many changes around here then."

"Really? They will be here that soon?"

"You had friends among the other ladies you are looking forward to seeing again?"

"Yes," I say, and I can feel my mood lighten. "Well, I had one. Yanmei. To see her again will bring me such joy."

Tao Fashi brushes my check. "Hold on to that feeling, my dear. You deserve a bit of happiness in your life."

Her well-meaning words send a pang through my heart. "Do I?"

She shakes her head. "Sometimes, it is you who is your worst enemy, Daiyu." She lets out a small groan as she stands, taking her little stool with her as she leaves me alone in the darkening courtyard.

As the light fades, so too does any joy I might have felt at Yanmei's arrival. Tao Fashi is right. I am my own enemy. I am the one who brings pain and suffering to those around me. Suyin was not here at the Temple of Grief for a full day before she was killed, mistaken for me. Will something terrible befall Yanmei when we meet again?

I crawl to my bed, exhausted in my body, heart, and mind, yet unable to find rest for any of them.

6

The next few days are a flurry of activity as we
prepare for the new arrivals. Of course, it should
be a somber time. The emperor is dead, after all. And yet,
the fact that so many new women will be coming to live
with us at the Temple of Grief is a change that happens so
very rarely. For most women here, their lives have been the
same, day in and day out, for decades. This is the only
opportunity most women here will have to meet new
people, make new friends.

Tao Fashi remains surprisingly calm as she directs all
the changes that must be made, but I can see in the lines of
her forehead, the twinge at the corner of her eye, that she is
anxious. I do what I can to be useful, making no complaints
as over a hundred additional beds are brought in and
arranged. In one building, there is no space between the
beds from wall to wall, and the women will have to crawl in
and out from the ends of them. Hundreds of new bowls and
chopsticks must be washed and put away, along with crates
and crates of food. A dozen more women are selected to
now serve in the kitchen to help prepare so much more

food. It seems that the temple's population is about to double, and I can hardly see how we will be able to accommodate everyone. But we will have to do our best, I suppose.

The day finally arrives, and I am nervous. I am excited to see Yanmei, but hesitant to see many of the other ladies. I was not well-liked within the harem, and I did little to reach out and be friendly to the other women. When I was the emperor's favorite and the empress, it was easy for me to keep myself apart. I had a large private home with tall walls and my own servants. I could pretend that my little household was all that existed within the great red walls of the Forbidden City. But here, within the Temple of Grief, all women, save Tao Fashi, are equals. We live together, sleep together, work together, side by side. How the ladies will react to seeing me here like this, I have no idea. They might find it amusing to see me brought so low. They might still hold resentment that I was once elevated above them. Or perhaps they will give no thought to my presence at all.

Neither am I looking forward to the adjustment period the ladies will have to go through. While some of the ladies were from low birth—for a Manchu—most were high-born. Most lived all their lives with servants, fine silk garments, and endless bowls of food and sweets at their fingertips. But here, there are no servants. Not everyone cooks, but we all wash our own bowls after we eat. We serve ourselves our meals. We wash our clothes and hang them to dry. We wash our own bodies from pails of water that we heat over a fire. Our clothes are simple and plain, as are our shoes. As widows, we are forbidden to paint our faces. Though, a few of the younger widows cannot seem to help put a little color on their cheeks and lips. As long as it is not ostentatious, Tao Fashi tends to look the other way. But as I look around now, I see that no one has taken liberty with their looks or done more than plait their hair. I wonder if Tao Fashi spoke to some of the women privately and asked them to set a good example for the new arrivals. I am sure—at least I hope—the ladies were informed about the rules of their new way of life before arriving, but actually having to live such a mean existence after a life of opulence will be difficult for many of the ladies, I am sure.

To say nothing of how young many of them are, as I am. Most still have decades of existence ahead of them, years that should be filled with love and children. Living in the harem, dozens of women bound to one man, was hard enough. But at least as wives to the emperor, there was a chance of gaining his affection, of having his children. But here, in this place devoid of men, that hope is gone. I know that Tao Fashi has many years of experience offering comfort to the women who are sent here, but I do not envy her task ahead. Many of the ladies are sure to be heartbroken, lost, hopeless. I do not know how they will find peace here...

I am sweeping the floor of one of the sleeping halls when someone announces that the ladies are coming. I place my broom against a wall and, for some reason, I smooth my hair and the front of my simple, orange, linen gown before stepping outside into the sun and making my way to the courtyard. Everyone is present, so I try to lose myself in the crowd, hopefully standing where I can see the new arrivals but not be seen.

In small groups of two or three, the ladies walk through our gate and are greeted by Tao Fashi. I am too far away to recognize anyone in particular at first, but they seem... bewildered, looking around with large and confused eyes. Whatever it was they were expecting, I am sure it was not this. After living in the palace, they probably thought that the temple they were being sent to would be not too dissimilar. Beautiful and well-appointed. They probably had no idea just how simple their new surroundings would be.

Tao Fashi welcomes the ladies, who in turn introduce themselves. One of Tao Fashi's assistants then checks a registry and tells them where their rooms are. I feel a shiver down my spine as I recall the similarity to my arrival at the Forbidden City. I had no idea what to expect, or what was expected of me. I was a name on a list, and nothing more. Oh, I know that to Tao Fashi, each lady matters. But still, for now, there is a process that must be adhered to, and it gives me chills.

Finally, I see a face I recognize, Euhmeh, and I shudder. Her chin is high, and she looks around, her eyes searching. I feel as though she is looking for me. I duck low behind the women in front of me, praying she does not see me. I would not say that Euhmeh and I were enemies, but we were never friends. I had attempted to reach out to her, asking that she help me with the harem accounts, but after some bad advice from Emperor Guozhi, a wedge was driven between us that I could not repair, though I did not try very hard to make amends. She grew closer to the dowager empress after that, which only made me more leery of her. I suddenly realize that the dowager empress will now be without many of her ladies-in-waiting, such as Euhmeh. That must make the loss of her son even more poignant. She has lost her son and her closest friends and confidants. Could that have something to do with why she tried to have me killed? Does Euhmeh know anything about the attempt on my life? The thought makes me shrink even deeper into myself and I crouch down, nearly to the ground, and wrap my arms around my knees. I wish the floor of the courtyard would open and swallow me whole, take me away from this place.

"Daiyu!" I hear Tao Fashi call out. The ladies around me take a step back and look down at me quizzically. I rise to my feet and brush myself off.

"Daiyu?" someone asks, a warm and familiar voice.

"Yes, she changed it to Daiyu when she came here."

I step through the crowd and the woman Tao Fashi is talking to turns to me, her face round, her smile wide.

"Lihua!" Yanmei says. She rushes to me and takes me in her arms. For a moment, I'm stunned. I knew she was coming, that she would be here, and yet, seeing her in person, hearing her voice, holding her in my arms, it is a shock to me.

"I'm so happy to see you," she says. "I missed you so much."

Finally, I let my body relax and let go of my fears and suspicions. I wrap my arms around her and hug her tightly. I want to tell her that I missed her too. That I love her. That having her here changes everything. But I can say nothing. My voice chokes and tears fall from my eyes. Somehow, I let out a small laugh. A laugh and a cry at the same time. Is this what people mean when they say they cry with happiness?

I do not know how long we hug, but it is Yanmei who pulls away first. She cups my cheeks and wipes away my tears.

"Look at you," she says. "You look so different."

"Do I?" I manage to croak.

She nods. "I mean that in a good way. You look...happy."

"Only because you are here," I say. I then take a step back and get a good look at her. I would not say that she looks good. Her face is pale and drawn, and she has always been a skinny girl. I run my hand over her forehead to check for a fever. "Are you ill?"

She takes my hand in hers and shakes her head. "No. But the last few months have not been easy. We have much to talk about."

"I am sure," I say. "Though Suyin told me—" My voice catches in my throat at the thought of my last friend who came to see me here in this place.

"Suyin?" Yanmei asks, her eyes wide. "She's here?"

I shake my head as my eyes fill with tears.

"Then where is she?" she asks.

I am too ashamed to reply.

"I'm so sorry," Yanmei says. My rough hands are trembling and cold as she takes them into her own, which are still warm and soft. She has not yet had months of hard work to make them rough. She wraps an arm around me and we walk away from the crowd to a more isolated part of the courtyard.

"When she disappeared, I hoped that she had found her way to you," she says. "I never imagined that she could have come to a bad end, and so quickly."

"She..." I do my best to find my voice. Yanmei deserves to know the truth. "She came here, and then she died in my arms."

"What?" Yanmei asks, recoiling slightly.

"I will tell you everything, I promise."

She presses her lips, but seems less sure of herself now. Perhaps she had tried to see the positives in coming here, in being with me, in being free of the red walls. But now, the reality of her situation is settling in. She is in a strange place with strange people, and it is not as safe as she thought it would be. The guilt chills me to the bone, and I wish I could send her away.

"There, there," Yanmei finally says, the smile returning to her face. "We are together now. All will turn out right, I promise."

I pull her back to me in a tight hug, which she returns eagerly. I can't change what happened to Suyin. I'd been foolish, complacent. I tried to pretend that the outside world couldn't affect me here. But I know better now.

This time, things will be different.

7

———

"The world is an unfair place," Yanmei says as she places flowers on Suyin's grave. "She was such a kind person, a loyal person. The dowager empress should pay for this."

"How?" I ask. "I could never prove that she was the person who sent the assassin."

"Unless you found the assassin," Yanmei says, but a coy lift to the corner of her mouth shows she is speaking in jest.

"I assume he will spend the rest of his life in hiding," I say. "The dowager surely would not allow him to live if she found him."

"At least you are safe for now," Yanmei says, walking away from the grave with her eyes to the ground, looking for nuts or herbs or other useful items to put into her basket.

"Am I?" I ask, following along.

"She surely will not try again," Yanmei says. "Especially with all of us here now."

"I don't know," I say, watching the woods around us warily. "She is a stubborn, determined woman."

"Yes, but her power is greatly diminished," Yanmei says, prying a nut open with her teeth to try and identify it. "The prince— I mean, *Emperor* Honghui cares for her not at all. He only allowed her to stay in the inner court because he had to. Officially, she is his mother, but it is clear to everyone that they don't like each other."

My heart hitches at the mention of Honghui. I'm so afraid that my feelings for him will be plain on my face that I've dared not ask about him. I turn away and seem very interested in some lichen on a nearby tree in an attempt to hide my face.

But I know the prince—the *emperor*—must be suffering so. He loved his brother very much. His own mother died when he was very young. Fenfeng should have loved him as she did her own son, but it was clear she did not. It is customary for an emperor's mother to serve as a sort of informal confidant and counselor. I know that Fenfeng fulfilled that role for Guozhi. It must grate on Fenfeng that Honghui does not hold her in the same estimation. But it is a situation of her own making. Had she loved him as a son, he would love her as a mother. As it is, they are stuck with one another until the bitter end.

"Had Honghui...chosen his empress?" I finally ask, though I still do not look directly at Yangmei as I do so. I keep my voice low, yet to my ears it echoes off the trees and bounces back to me loud as thunder.

Yanmei seems to not take note of the significance of my question, but just shakes her head. "I think he's been too preoccupied to even think about taking a wife. He's been effectively serving as emperor ever since Guozhi was injured."

"I suppose he won't be able to ignore the issue now," I say. "There will be a consort selection again."

Yanmei surprises me with a snorting laugh. "If there are any eligible girls left. Our selection was so recent."

"True," I say. "But some of us were chosen based on our birth numbers. Many were probably dismissed for the same reason. Girls who were not compatible with Guozhi might be compatible with Honghui."

"Oh, you're right," Yanmei says. "I wonder what the court astrologers will be looking for this time around."

"I have no idea," I say. Of course, I didn't know what they were looking for last time either. Mingxia did, which was why she was so determined to find a stand-in for her own daughter, Lihua.

"I suppose it doesn't matter," Yanmei says. "It won't be either of us this time." She turns back toward the abbey, swinging her basket alongside her in a carefree sort of way. She has only been here a couple of days but seems to be adjusting remarkably well. Many of the girls cry themselves to sleep. More than a couple have run away. Tao Fashi is supposed to report any runaways immediately, but I have a feeling she is taking her time in doing so. Some women are not meant for this life. One young woman committed suicide by hanging herself inside the main temple. Some of the ladies now refuse to go in there for fear of meeting her vengeful ghost. But Yanmei has taken everything in stride. She has been kind and helpful and so encouraging to me. She is far more resilient than I ever gave her credit for in the past.

But I still have not told her the truth about me, who I really am. I've tried. I've opened my mouth to spill out everything, but only silence escapes my throat. I want to tell her, truly. I fear that I can never be a real friend to her unless she knows who I really am.

But I am a coward, as usual. Though, I do not merely

fear for myself. I do not think that Yanmei would share my secret or reject me for it. But after what happened to Suyin, I am terrified of something happening to Yanmei. If I were to reveal myself to Yanmei and then she was to die, I'm not sure I could bear it. Perhaps I am paranoid. As Yanmei said, surely the assassin will not return. Still, just to be safe, I have refused to let Yanmei sleep in the same building as me. She was surprised at first, and I think a little hurt, but after I told her about Suyin, she understood my reasons. I am sure she will also understand my reasons for staying silent for so long about who I really am. At least for waiting this long. The longer I wait, the less sure I can be on that account. Perhaps I should just tell her now.

"Yanmei, I—"

"Shh!" she says, holding up a hand as she listens intently. "Do you hear that?"

My heart beats so hard that at first, I can hear only the blood rushing in my ears. I look around frantically, waiting for the assassin to burst out of the woods, charging toward me, his dagger raised. When I see nothing of the sort, my ears clear enough for me to hear the thrumming on the ground of horse hooves—dozens of horse hooves.

"Someone is coming!" Yanmei says. "Lots of someones!" She takes off at a run back for the abbey. I follow behind with less urgency. The last time a rider came to the abbey, he had come to tell us that the emperor had died. No rider ever comes to the abbey carrying good news.

When we reach the path that leads to the abbey, we are both surprised to see more than a dozen imperial horses. All the horses bear a single rider, an imperial guard, both man and horse clad in armor and red silk. There is one horse at the head of them all, though, that bears no rider and is clad in yellow silk. Last time, the messenger came alone. Why would this messenger require a whole contingent of guards?

"What is happening?" Yanmei asks of no one in particular, for I certainly don't know. We then notice a loud commotion coming from the abbey. Crying, screaming, praying. Yanmei grips my arm and takes a step back. She looks at me as if to ask if we should run. If we should hide. I can understand her fear. What could be happening up at the abbey? Surely an imperial force would not arrive to do us harm. But what could have the ladies so stirred up?

I take another look at the riderless horse. The single, riderless horse. A whole cavalcade of men, but only one entered the abbey. This one alone adorned with yellow silk embroidered with five-toed dragons. My heart soars and I move toward the abbey without thinking.

"Wait!" Yanmei calls out to me, but I do not. If anything, I run faster. The men on their horses start when they see me, and I hear them murmur among themselves, but I do not pause to understand what they are saying.

I hold up the hem of my robe as I climb the stone steps to the abbey two at a time. And yet, I feel as though I am not running fast enough. I feel as though by the time I reach the abbey, the rider will be gone.

I trip when I reach the top step. It always has stuck out a little more than the others. From my position on my knees, I can only see a flurry of orange robes. The ladies have all gathered in the courtyard, many pushing and shoving one another to get a better look at the visitor, who I have no hope of seeing from my place on the ground.

I scramble to my feet and elbow my way through the crowd. A few of the ladies push back or stand firm, not wanting to yield their precious spot. But when they see that it is me who is trying to get through the crowd, most step aside, though with a hateful glare or a curse under their breath.

Finally, I see him. Prince Honghui. No. *Emperor* Honghui. He looks exactly how I remember him, but also completely different. He has the same beautiful face, but now it is heavy with burdens he was never meant for. He has the same tall, broad-shouldered body, but he carries himself with a more regal bearing somehow. I think that this is what it must mean to truly be noble. It is innate, something I never had, was never meant to have.

When our eyes meet, I want to run to him, jump into his arms, hold him. Kiss him. I feel drawn to him, like a moth to a flame, and I think he feels the same way. But we cannot go to one another. We must restrain our true feelings. No one can ever know that we have loved each other since long before his brother's death.

Finally, I remember my place and fall to my knees, touching my forehead to the ground in a kowtow. I am no one now. Not an empress. A mere commoner, banished to live out my days as a nun, while he is the emperor of China. When my head touches the ground, it is as if the shock of his arrival wears off and all the other ladies follow my lead, bowing before their emperor.

Even though my nose is to the dusty ground of the courtyard, my eyes are open and I can see the emperor step in front of me.

"I have been told that your name is Daiyu now," Honghui says.

I sit up on my heels but keep my eyes downcast. "Yes, Your Majesty," I say. "Does it please you?"

Honghui chuckles and extends his hand down to me. "Everything about you pleases me," he says brazenly as he pulls me to my feet. I feel my face blush, but I can think of nothing to say that won't scandalize those around us.

"Come," he says, tugging me toward the main temple where the large statue of Guanyin stands. "I must speak with you..."

8

———

"**Y**ou want me to do what?" I ask in shock. Surely what Prince Honghui— I mean, *Emperor* Honghui—just proposed was merely a figment of my imagination. He can't really have just asked me—

"Marry me," he says again. Still, I have to blink and shake my head. This must all be a dream.

"I don't understand," I say. "I was your brother's wife. I was banished, punished. I was told I had to spend the rest of my life here. How can I be your wife?"

We stand in the shadow of Guanyin, the doors to the temple shut tight so that we can speak privately. Still, there are windows open to let in some light and air, so we still stand some feet apart, a proper distance, just in case anyone tries to eavesdrop. It is difficult. I want nothing more than to be held tightly, safely, in his arms. But his words have so shocked me, I am near to toppling over.

"In his attempt to punish you," Emperor Honghui says, "my brother inadvertently freed you. According to court records, you don't exist. You never did exist. You were never married to Emperor Guozhi."

I suppose he is right. That was what the emperor said, that I was to be erased. I suppose I didn't think the erasure was literal. Or at least, not complete. Surely there must be a record of my erasure. Of my punishment. Could it be that I was really erased from all court records?

"So, because I was banished and erased, you want to marry me yourself?" I ask. "But I was your brother's wife. Doesn't that bother you?"

"It didn't bother me while he was alive," he says with a shrug. I feel a little nauseous at the thought. I didn't love the emperor, but was forced to accept him as my husband. It never bothered me overmuch that I was not faithful to him. But Honghui was Guozhi's brother. He should have known better, been more loyal than that. But Honghui loved me. I think, perhaps, he loved me even more than I loved him. I suppose that excused his actions in his own mind. And am I not alive because of those actions? He saved me when the foreigners stormed into the Forbidden City because he loved me.

"The official court records might have forgotten me," I say, "but people will remember. The servants, the court officials, Guozhi's mother. All of them will know who I am. Will they not take offense? Surely they will see wrong in it."

"There is precedent," Honghui says. I look at him dumbly. I don't understand what he means, but I feel as though this is something an educated Manchu lady should know, so I stay quiet.

"There have been instances in history when emperors have taken the wife of another as their own," he says, sensing my unease with the topic. "You have surely heard of Yang Guifei, one of the great beauties of the past."

"Umm...of course," I mumble even though I haven't the slightest idea who he is talking about.

"She was the wife of the emperor's son before the emperor took her for himself," he says. "Many people forget that part of the story. In fact, he sent her away to a nunnery for a while before he claimed her as his own. As the emperor, it is my right to choose you."

My heart flutters at that, at the thought of Emperor Honghui choosing me out of all the other women in the empire. He could have a younger wife, a prettier wife, a virgin wife. But instead, he wants me. And didn't I once think that if I could have the freedom to choose my own husband, I would choose him?

"Are you sure this is the right thing to do?" I ask. "It might be your right to choose me, but many people will be unhappy about this. Guozhi's mother, for one. And what about all the parents in the country who are hoping their daughter will be chosen as the next empress? It could cost you important allies."

"I don't care what Fenfeng thinks," Honghui nearly spits. "If I could send *her* here to this nunnery, I would. That woman has never been a mother to me.

"As for the people... Well, more people will be glad of our marriage than angered by it."

"What do you mean?" I ask.

Honghui sighs and takes a moment to respond. "There are many people, Han people, who are still angry at how Guozhi handled the foreign invasion, among other things. There is open talk of revolt, they aren't even hiding it anymore! I have had to send troops all over the country to put down rebels, and more are talking of rebellion every day. The people don't want a Manchu ruler anymore."

I cross my arms and can't help but smirk a little. For a moment, I remember living in the hutong outside the Forbidden City and hearing the people talk against the

Manchu. Blame them for our constant troubles, our poverty. Dream of once again seeing a Han Chinese emperor on the throne. Of seeing Han girls living lives of pleasure and opulence within the inner court. Of their families being showered with power and riches.

"There," Honghui says, pointing at me.

"What?" I ask.

"That...affinity you have for the Han people, it's plain on your face."

"Is it?" I ask innocently.

"The people see it too," he says. "They *have* seen it. They still talk about how you fed them and protected them while the court was in exile. How you put their well-being ahead of that of the court.

"They talk about how you alone rode back to the Forbidden City and offered yourself to the foreigners in exchange for ending the invasion."

"That's not exactly what happened," I say.

"But it is what the people think," Honghui says. "It's what they believe. They believe that you are the only Manchu noble in all of China who cares about them."

"Perhaps they are not wrong," I say.

"That's not fair," Honghui says. "I care about all my subjects."

I shrug. "I don't know. I haven't seen you as a ruler. I know that Guizhou only did what was best for the people in as much as it helped him. He didn't give food to the poor because they needed it. He did it to keep them from revolting. And it sounds like you have inherited his same attitude."

Honghui is stunned into silence for a moment. "Why do you *care* so much?" he finally asks, running his hand along the side of his head as if he would pull his hair out in frustration. "You think we should just give away money and food and clothes for no reason to people who would gladly kill us."

"It's not for no reason," I say. "As the Son of Heaven, it is your responsibility to care for your subjects as a father would his children. A father would not let his children starve." My eyes tear up at the memory of so many nights I couldn't sleep because I was so hungry. I know that it killed my father to see his children starve. He worked so hard to provide for us, but it was never enough.

"The Han Chinese outnumber the Manchu a hundred to one," I go on, practically yelling. "They could easily overthrow you...us. You rule at their pleasure, even if they don't really know it. If you do not take care of them, why should they allow you to remain on the throne? They will replace you if you do not do right by them."

Honghui is silent for a long while. I think he is waiting to see if I am done speaking. Of course, there is more I could say, so very much more, but I do not. I hold my tongue. If I keep talking, I may end up revealing more than I should.

"This is why I need you to marry me," Honghui says. "The people, somehow, know that you support them. That you will fight for them. I believe that if you marry me, it will go a long way toward calming their anger at the court and at me."

I am taken a little aback at this. "You think that marrying me will help save the court?"

"I do," he says. "Think of it as a political marriage, one that will unite two warring factions. You and I can save the Qing Dynasty."

"Is that the real reason you wish to marry me?" I ask. "To save your throne?"

Honghui chuckles and walks over to me. He tugs on my robe, pulling me to him. "That is merely a bonus," he says, wrapping an arm around me and lowering his voice. "Think of it, my darling, being able to openly love one another. No longer having to sneak around and make love in dark and hidden places for fear of being caught."

The thought of making love to Honghui makes my belly quiver and I feel the instant pang of desire in the deepest parts of myself.

"Well...I enjoyed making love in dark and hidden places," I admit sheepishly.

Honghui turns me to him and places his lips on mine, hungrily, eagerly. Even though the windows are open and we are sure to be seen, I wrap my hand around his neck and kiss him back.

"Perhaps we could still steal away to our favorite places," he whispers, "late at night, when no one is watching."

"I'd like that," I say. We kiss again, and for a moment, it's so easy to pretend that everything is perfect. That everything is just how it should be. But life is never that simple, at least for me. I finally pull away and take a few steps back.

"There are a few things I must ask of you," I say, "if I am to agree to this...arrangement of yours."

"Oh?" Honghui asks, his eyebrow cocked. "Making demands of me?"

"No," I say. "Or maybe yes. But marrying me will not help your reputation with the Han if nothing changes."

He nods slowly. "I suppose that is true. Go on."

"When you select new consorts, you must significantly limit the number of women you choose."

"Want me all to yourself, do you?" he asks playfully. I know he only means to tease me, but his words hurt and insult me.

"I am not a jealous woman," I say. "I understand the role consorts play in the greater scheme of things. But the inner court is a massive waste of funds. I want some of the money that would be spent on consorts to be given out in poor relief instead."

"Yes, I know you were quite passionate about that when you were merely one of my brother's consorts," Honghui says. "And I suppose it is one of the things that endeared you to the people in the first place, so it is something we should keep going. Anything else?"

"You should appoint Han men to court positions," I say. "How can you possibly make decisions on behalf of people you don't know? You need Han men at your side, advising you."

He rubs his chin at the thought. "That will be difficult. Some of the other ministers will not like it."

"Then replace them with men who will," I say. "You need the Han by your side if you wish to convince them that you have their best interests at heart."

"Very well," he says. "I will see what I can do. What else?"

I chew my lower lip for a moment. "There is one thing I would ask for myself. Dongmei and Jiangfei, I wish to be appointed as their mother, and me alone. I'll not have Fenfeng interfere with their upbringing."

"Consider it done," he says. "Dongmei... Well, she needs you. Misses you."

I feel a pang in my heart. I miss the girls so much. But I know they must be hurting. I promised them, time and again, that I would not leave them, and yet we were always ripped apart. I can only hope they will accept me back into their lives one more time.

"Anything else?" he asks.

"Yes," I say. "Lady Yanmei must be allowed to return with me as my lady-in-waiting," I say. "I'll not leave her here."

"Very well. And I will return all your old household staff to you as well, your maids and eunuchs. How would that be?"

"I would appreciate that," I say, though I am saddened that Suyin will not be among them. Oh, if only she had stayed at the Forbidden City and not come here to me, she would still be alive and we would be reunited! The world is truly a cruel and unfair place.

"Anything else?" Honghui asks.

I shake my head. "Not that I can think of at the moment. But this is all rather sudden. I never imagined that I would be allowed to return to the Forbidden City. That I would marry you. That I would be the empress again."

Honghui holds his hand out to me, and I take it. "Let us hope that our lives are much easier from here on out. That we may have a time of peace and prosperity."

"I pray it is so," I say.

9

The next morning, before the sun rises, I mount a horse to return to the Forbidden City. I have told no one that I am leaving, save Tao Fashi and Yanmei. I know that the other ladies who only just arrived will be shocked, hurt, and angry that I am being allowed to leave, to return to our shared home, while they must stay behind. But I am a coward and cannot face them. There is nothing I can do to lessen their pain, their jealousy, except perhaps turn Honghui away, and I would be a fool to do that. No, I cannot save them, help them, but I can help myself and Yanmei, and that will have to be enough.

"May the blessings of Guanyin go with you, my girl," Tao Fashi says, kissing my forehead goodbye.

"Thank you for everything," I say. "These many months would have been unbearable without your guidance.

"The road ahead will not be easy, I fear," Tao Fashi says, her face grim.

I can only shrug. "My life has never been easy. But I believe I will have more opportunities to do good when I am back in Peking. Perhaps I can even correct some of the mistakes of my past."

"I will pray for you constantly," Tao Fashi says, her eyes watering. We hug for the last time, and then I mount my horse before I lose my composure, sitting tall next to Honghui.

Instead of riding back to the Forbidden City hidden away inside a sedan chair, Honghui wishes for all the people we pass to be able to see me. He wants it to be known that the empress that the people love so dearly has returned. Yanmei, however, rides inside my chair to protect her fair skin from the sun and wind.

I have shed my orange nun garb and instead wear the red robe of a bride. Honghui had suggested that I wear the imperial yellow of an empress, but when I enter the Forbidden City this time, I want it to be as a bride for Honghui, not Guozhi's empress. I never loved Guozhi, never wanted to be his woman. It was never my choice to be summoned to this bed. The fact that he was kind to me, good to me even, does not negate the fact that he had bought me like a sack of rice.

This time, things are different. Honghui didn't order me to marry him—he asked me. It was the first time in my life I was asked to do anything. Of course, Mingxia asked me to take her daughter's place at the consort selection. She hadn't forced me to do so. But could I really have said no when she offered me so much money? Money that could save my family from starving? I couldn't say no, and Mingxia knew that. I wonder for a moment where she and Lihua are. Is Lihua happy? Did she take advantage of her freedom and marry for love? I suppose I'll never know.

A sense of relief washes over me as we enter Peking. I'm home. People bow at the emperor as we pass, but slowly, whispers ripple through the crowds and people look up, even though their faces are downcast. They are looking at me.

"Is that the empress?" they ask one another. I meet their curious eyes and smile, giving knowing nods.

"Empress! Empress!" It is the children who dare acknowledge me first. They run alongside my horse, waving, laughing.

"It is the empress!" I hear people say. "The empress has returned!" The voices race ahead of us so that people start to watch our approach with anticipation. When they catch sight of me, they clap and cheer. Parents hold their children high so that they may catch a glimpse of me.

"See," Honghui says, "they still love you."

My heart swells. I feel as though I have done so little for them, certainly not enough to engender such love and devotion. But, considering how little the Manchu have done over the past centuries for the Han people, I suppose even my small acts of kindness must have seemed bountiful. Even a single grain of rice can seem like a feast to a starving person.

"If you give them money," I say, "they will love you too."

"What?" Honghui says. "Just throw money at them for no reason?"

"Is not earning the goodwill of your people reason enough?" I ask. He looks at me as if I am an annoying child, but then he sighs and unties a purse from his belt. He opens the purse and offers the coins inside to me.

"After you," he says.

I reach inside the purse and pull out a handful of coins. I take a coin in my right hand and lean down, reaching toward a woman with a baby on her hip. Our fingers touch and the coin slides from my hand to hers. Her eyes widen in surprise, and I only catch a glimpse of the joy on her face before the long strides of my horse leave her far behind me. But I can hear her voice call after me.

"Thank you, Empress!" she yells. "May you live ten thousand years!"

I try to move more quickly, passing the coins into hands waiting merely to touch me, not expecting to receive money simply for stepping aside from the wide road as we pass. They thank me, praise me, drop to their knees in gratitude.

Suddenly, a face appears in the crowd. A face of know. A face I remember. As he walks toward me, I lean out even further and reach for him. But as he gets closer, I realize that it's not who I think it is.

It's not my father. I blink hard, letting the tears that had threatened to fall clear the dust away that must have been clouding my vision. The man does look similar to my father —middle-aged, wiry, long hair grayed before its time by decades of exhausting labor. But it is not him. Still, I see my father in him. I see my mother in the woman next to him, and my sisters in the children that run around their feet. I give the man the remainder of the coins from my purse.

"Heaven bless you, Empress," he says, and it is as if I can hear my father's voice. I feel as though he is not speaking only for himself, but for all the Han people.

The gates of Forbidden City loom before us, and to my surprise, they open. I tug on my horse's reins to slow her down. I expect to be directed around the wall so that I may enter through the east or west gates, as I always have before. I am only a woman, after all.

Honghui notices that I am lagging behind and he motions for me to catch up. "You are the empress," he says. "You come this way."

I gulp as I tentatively urge my horse forward. I

remember something from my previous time here about empresses being the only women allowed to enter the Forbidden City from the main gate, and only on their wedding day. I know that this is my right, but it still feels... wrong, somehow. I then remember that Honghui still does not know the truth about me. That I am not Manchu.

I have played the part for so long, I almost forgot myself that I am not who I am pretending to be. I know that I have already agreed to Emperor Honghui's proposal. That marriage to me is important to him and his position as emperor. But it has all been based on a lie. I had thought that my marriage to Honghui would be different from my marriage to Guozhi. That it would be better because it is my choice. Because we love each other. But can it truly be better if it is still based on the same lie?

"Honghui," I say. He looks at me. I open my mouth, but a loud booming sound like an explosion drowns out my words. But it was not an explosion. I look back and see that the big red gates have slammed closed behind us.

"Hmm?" Honghui looks at me expectantly.

I sigh and shake my head. "Nothing." I'm here now. I cannot back out without hurting him, hurting myself, hurting Yanmei. Perhaps I have made a mistake. Perhaps I should not have returned. But it is too late to change things now.

"Are you sure?" Honghui asks me. "You look as though you are facing down an executioner."

I try to gulp, but the phlegm gets stuck in my throat. I had forgotten about the seriousness of my deception until now. I don't think that Honghui would have me put to death if he learned the truth about me, but Guozhi could have. That is one way in which Honghui and Guozhi differ from one another. Honghui is gentle and sensitive while Guozhi was strict and rigid. I'll never forget that Guozhi sent Lady An to her death without cause. Honghui never would have done such a cruel thing.

I shake my head and force a smile. "I just never thought I would return here, especially as an empress."

Honghui chuckles as he jumps down from his horse. He then reaches up, putting his hands on my waist as he lowers me to my feet. Our bodies brush together, and I feel a fluttering in my stomach. Even though we have been reunited for days, we have yet to consummate our new roles as husband and wife. Each day of the journey was exhausting and left us filthy with dust and sweat and horse stink. I was able to wash my body each night with creek water boiled in a kettle over a fire, but it seemed to do little for my aching bones, nor could I wash my hair. While I am still tired from the journey, I know that a long soak in a tub with perfumed soaps and oils awaits me. Once my hair and body are clean and my aching muscles relaxed, I know that I will be more than eager to lay with my husband. And the knowledge that our relationship will no longer need to be kept secret increases rather than diminishes my desire.

"May I come to your room tonight, Your Majesty?" I ask him.

"I thought you'd never ask," he says, pulling me to him and kissing me in full view of all those around us. I hear gasps and the uncomfortable shuffling of feet. It is not common for any couple to show affection in public, much less an emperor and empress. I feel Honghui's fingers dig into my back and his breath shudders.

"Must we wait?" he asks me.

I chuckle. "Everything should be done properly," I say. "We don't want to give anyone cause to object to our marriage."

He sighs in disappointment. "Of course." His fingers slowly release me, though reluctantly. As he does so, I see a large group of servants approaching, at the head of which are my former chief eunuch, Jinhai, and senior maid, Nuwa. When they reach me, Jinhai drops to this knees and bursts into tears.

"My lady!" he cries. "My most kind and generous lady. I have missed you so much. I thought I would never see you again."

"Nor I you, my friend," I say, kneeling down and lightly tugging on his shoulders to encourage him to stand.

"I wanted to go to you," he says, wiping his face with his sleeves, "go with Suyin. But I knew I would never be permitted to enter the temple."

"I know," I say. "Suyin told me."

"You...you saw her? Talked to her?" he says, confusion and hope in his voice as he looks around. I then notice that Yanmei is among those gathered, even though she would have had to enter the Forbidden City through a side gate. If Suyin had returned with us, she most likely would have entered with Yanmei. When Jinhai realizes that Suyin is not among us, he looks at me, daring to look me directly in the face.

"Where is she?" he asks, and I can hear the fear in his voice of the answer. I can feel tears welling up in my eyes as I watch his face crumble.

"I'm sorry," is all I can say.

"No," he says as he slumps back to the ground, a puddle at my feet. I kneel down and do my best to comfort him, but I know there is little comfort to be had. Suyin and Jinhai had been by my side from the day I first entered the Forbidden City. Together, they worked to raise me up from the lowest-ranked concubine to an empress. They were friends and partners. Losing Suyin must feel like losing a sister to Jinhai.

"Please, someone take him somewhere he can rest," I say.

"No!" Jinhai says, forcing himself to his feet. "I—I must attend to my duties, to you, my lady."

I take his hands in mine and squeeze them. "Having you back by my side is more than enough."

He bows and thanks me. "I must make sure your palace is ready for your arrival." He shuffles off, along with half a dozen of the servants who had come to greet me. Nuwa then steps to my side and offers me her arm. I take it gladly, even though I do not need her assistance for walking since I am not wearing pot-bottom shoes, but leather slippers more appropriate for riding a horse.

"Welcome home, my lady," Nuwa says, and my heart swells at the thought of finally being able to truly call this place my home.

10

"Have the girls brought to me," I tell Nuwa as we make our way to my palace. "I have missed them so much. I wrote to them… Well, I had a letter written to them every week that I was away. Tell me, did they receive any of them?"

Nuwa presses her lips into a thin line. "That was very thoughtful of you, my lady. But surely, you must have known that it would be a wasted effort. The dowager empress would never have allowed the girls to see them."

"I was afraid it would be so," I say. "But I still do not think the effort was wasted. It is important to me that the girls know that I did not forget them during my time away. That I would never forget them. That I did not abandon them."

Nuwa is quiet for a moment, then she forces a smile to her lips. "Yes, my lady. Of course."

"What is it?" I ask her.

She shakes her head. "Nothing, Your Majesty. You are right in everything, of course."

I stop and turn to face her. Nuwa does not look

directly at me. "Do you think I keep you by my side to lie to me? I do not wish for you to ply me with lies and sweet words. Tell me the truth. What have I done wrong?" Now that Suyin is gone, Nuwa is the woman I will have to rely on to help me, protect me even, here in the palace. I care for Nuwa greatly, and I think she wants what is best for me, but we are not as close as I was with Suyin. No one in the world is like Suyin. But without Suyin, Nuwa and I will need to come to a new understanding, develop a new sort of relationship, one in which I can trust her completely.

"I do not lie to you, my lady," she says firmly. "You did nothing wrong. But you must understand that the girls are too young to understand all that has happened. They are hurt and angry. And the fact that the dowager kept your letters from them..." She shakes her head. "I'm sorry. I only want you to be prepared."

"Be prepared for what?" I ask.

She sighs. "The girls... They have not been themselves since you left. Dongmei in particular. They have been angry. Rebellious. Even the dowager cannot control them, it seems."

"Well, I can hardly blame them. They had two mothers in Lady An and Empress Caihong, and they lost both of them in a matter of months. Then they lost me as well, more than once. They lost their father. They must feel so alone, afraid of what will be taken away from them next."

"Indeed, my lady," Nuwa says. "They have suffered so much in their short lives."

"Still, have them brought to my palace. I will see them as soon as possible," I say. "I am the empress now, Honghui's full, proper, and only wife. I'm not going anywhere again."

"Yes, my lady," Nuwa says with a bow. She then motions toward the open gate of my palace.

I shake my head. "No, I am going to see the dowager first."

"Now?" Nuwa says, alarm on her face. "But...you are not dressed!"

I chuckle. "I am hardly naked," I say, indicating my red wedding gown.

"You know what I mean," Nuwa says, not amused. "You are travel-worn. Filthy. Your hair..." She shakes her head. "No, you cannot see your mother-in-law this way. She will not respect you."

"She won't respect me anyway," I say. "Besides, I see no reason to waste time and energy making myself beautiful for her. Who is she to me?"

Nuwa worries her hands together. "Perhaps... But, oh, my lady. Are you sure? You would feel so much better after you had a bath and your hair combed—"

"Later," I say, and I make my way toward the dowager empress's palace. I want to see the old woman, now, before I lose any of my anger toward her. And before she has more time to plot against me. By now, she has surely heard of my return, but she won't be expecting me to visit her so soon. She was probably planning on coming to my palace on her own, to "pay her respects." She would have been dressed in her finest clothes, followed by her entire household, all in an attempt to intimidate me. But I no longer fear her. What can she do to me? She only held power before because she was Guozhi's mother. Whether or not he loved her, I cannot say. He never intimated to me that he did. In fact, there were many times that he sided with me over her. But he did at least honor her as his mother, and he expected me to do the same. But Guozhi is gone, and Honghui feels none of the respect toward her that his brother did. Dowager empress Fenfeng might still reside within the palace walls, but she might as well not exist anymore considering the lack of power or respect she now commands.

In addition to Nuwa, around half a dozen servants, maids and eunuchs, follow me. One of the eunuchs runs ahead and announces my arrival at Fenfeng's palace. When I step through the gate into her courtyard, it is as I suspected. The place is in a flurry of activity as maids and eunuchs rush to either bow before me or attempt to escape my notice to finish their tasks for Fenfeng. A moment later, Fenfeng appears from her bed chamber looking more haggard than I have ever seen her. It seems I caught her in the middle of dressing as she still wears flat slippers and her hair is merely pulled back, a headdress attached to her head slightly askew. I cannot suppress a pleased smile at having caught her off guard.

"Mother," I say sweetly. "It is good to see you again."

"Indeed, Empress," Fenfeng says from her kneeling position before me. A position that I know must be painful for her old knees, but I do not give her leave to stand. "Your return is a joyous surprise."

I chuckle, but there is little humor in it. "It must have been more of a surprise to you than most, considering the... guest you sent to visit me a few weeks ago."

Fenfeng is quiet for a moment. Surely my hint about the assassin was not that vague.

"I know not what you mean," she says.

My heart skips a beat and my confidence falters. Could I have been wrong? Was she not the person who sent the assassin after me?

"Though..." she continues, rising from kneeling without my permission, "I did hear that your little servant went to visit you." She looks directly at my face. "Is that who you are referring to?"

My mouth goes dry. So, I was right. She did send the man to kill me. And, somehow, she knows that he killed Suyin instead. Could it be that she sent the assassin to kill Suyin in the first place? Was she merely sending me a message? Telling me that she was never beyond her reach. Telling me that I would never be safe? Could I truly have underestimated her so much?

I do not know what to say about any of this. I wasn't prepared. I'm not as smart, as quick on my feet, as Fenfeng is. I decide to change the subject.

"Give me the letters," I say.

"What letters?" she asks.

"The letters I wrote to the girls every week that I was at the Temple of Grief," I say.

"I don't know what you are talking about," she says.

"I know you kept them," I say, clenching my hands into fists. "I knew when I wrote them that you would never let the girls see them, but I wrote to them anyway, such is my love for them. Now, give them back to me!"

"I burned them!" Fenfeng says, showing more emotion than I expected.

"How dare you," I hiss.

"How dare you!" Fenfeng replies. "You don't know those girls. You don't really love them. You weren't there when they were born. You haven't been here to watch them grow into women. You were banished. Erased. For you to write them, to pretend you still had some part to play in their lives, was cruel. Why give them false hope of even seeing you again? You should have stayed at the abbey and stayed silent like you were told to do!"

My mouth gapes, but I am unable to respond. I wrote to

the girls because I loved them... But is Fenfeng right? Would my letters have done more harm than good? She is right to an extent. I never thought I would be back here, that I would see them again. That I would have a chance at being their mother again. But...but I *am* here. I did return.

"You're wrong," I tell Fenfeng, and I think my words shock her. I've never been brave enough to stand up to her before. "Perhaps I didn't know that I would return, but I did. You are the one who hurt the girls by letting them lose hope. By letting them think that I had abandoned and forgotten them."

"I did what was best for them," Fenfeng says.

"You did what was best for *you*," I say. "You wanted them to lose hope. You wanted them to think that you were the only woman in the world who loved and cared for them. You don't love them. You don't know what it means to love. You only love yourself."

Fenfeng's face twists in rage, her teeth grinding, her eyes hard. Her nostrils flare and I think I hear her growl. I brace myself for the coming barrage of hateful words, but slowly, her face relaxes. She leans back and stretches her neck, a sense of calm washing over her. Then she laughs.

"You always were a foolish child," she says, and I hear her servants snicker all around me. I feel terribly embarrassed and wish only to run away.

"You have only every play-acted at being empress," Fenfeng goes on. "You have no idea what it truly means to be the mother of an emperor. The wife of an emperor. To raise princesses. To have the fate of an empire resting on your shoulders.

"You speak of love as if it is the only emotion that matters. You forget that duty, honor, and loyalty are far more important. Love is fleeting. Love is weak. Love dies.

Love means nothing." She sneers at me. "You will never be a real empress."

"The emperor would disagree with you," I say.

"I've outlived three emperors," she says with a smirk, "and I'm not going anywhere."

"We'll see about that," is all I can think to say. An empty threat, I know. Honghui has no intention of sending her away. And if I were to ask him to do so, I do not know how he would react. By marrying me, he has already taken a great risk at bucking tradition. I do not think he would go further by ousting his mother figure.

There is nothing more I can think to say to the woman, so I turn and leave her courtyard. I can hear the dowager, and all her servants, laugh boisterously as I exit. Soon, all of the Forbidden City will know that I made a fool of myself before the dowager empress. I should have known better than attempt to confront her. She is smarter than me. Older. Wiser. And far more dangerous.

I had thought that I was safe in my new position, but I could be in more danger than ever before.

11

———

 y the time I finally make it back to my palace, the little princesses, Jiangfei and Dongmei, are there waiting for me. I open my arms as I go to them, expecting us to be reunited in a loving hug. But the girls seem altogether uninterested in my presence. They do not come toward me, nor do they hug me back when I take them into my arms.

It has only been six months since I last saw them, but they both now seem so much older than their five and seven years of age. Dongmei seems especially sullen, hardly looking me in the face when I speak to her. Jiangfei looks at me with both fear and longing, as though she is afraid to love me because I will abandon her again.

I have no plans to ever leave them again, but I did not want to leave them in the past either. I do not believe anyone can foretell the future perfectly. Who knows what may happen tomorrow?

"Dongmei, Jiangfei," I say, kneeling down so that I can look them in the eyes and they can see my sincerity. "I am so sorry that I was away for so long. I missed you so much."

The girls shift uncomfortably on their feet and say nothing.

"I understand if you are angry with me," I try. "I promised you that I would never leave you, but I did. It wasn't my choice to go, but I still abandoned you. I'm so sorry for that, and I will do my best to make it up to you."

"So...you are staying this time?" Jiangfei tentatively asks.

Dongmei shoots her an angry look, and I wonder if the girls made some sort of secret agreement ahead of time to not speak to me.

"Your uncle, Honghui, is the emperor now," I say, even though they already know this much. "He has chosen me to be his empress. I'm not going anywhere."

"You've been the empress before," Dongmei says. "You were Baba's empress. But he sent you away. Emperor Honghui could do the same thing."

Dongmei was always so smart. I'm honestly surprised she hasn't figured out the whole truth about me yet. Unfortunately, her wide eyes have shown her ugly truths about the world that would be better left unseen.

"You are right," I say to her. "Being empress does not mean I can't possibly be sent away again."

Jiangfei sniffles and wipes at her eyes with her sleeves.

"I'm sorry," I say, growing frustrated with myself. "I'm saying everything wrong. I only mean that nothing in this world is certain. But I am going to do everything within my power to stay right here in the Forbidden City for the rest of my life. That, at least, I can promise you."

I wait anxiously for their response, hoping that they will find it in their hearts to forgive me and snuggle into my arms. But they only look at each other for a moment, and then Dongmei shrugs, as if the two of them are having a silent conversation.

"May we go now?" Dongmei asks me. "I have a painting lesson."

I feel as though my heart is struck through with an arrow. It takes all my willpower to not cry, to beg for their forgiveness. Instead, I nod, chewing on my lower lip to try and keep myself steady.

"Of course," I manage to choke out, but it is little more than a whisper. Both girls then turn away and are escorted back to their own palace. I stand and the tears I had been holding back flow freely as soon as they are out of sight. Nuwa puts her arms around my shoulders to comfort me.

"They are never going to forgive me," I sob.

"Of course they will," Nuwa says, pulling out an embroidered handkerchief and dabbing at my face with it. "Just give them time."

I nod and let her lead me inside the palace. My stomach rumbles at the smells wafting from my private kitchen. I eat and fill up much too quickly, leaving countless bowls of food untouched. Then, Nuwa draws me a bath. I am embarrassed by how filthy the water becomes, gray as mud. I fear that not all the dirt has come from days on the road, but from months of not being able to completely wash myself. She has to gently pick out all the knots that have formed in my hair. After what feels like hours, I am washed, oiled, and perfumed, and I feel like a different person. I feel like an empress.

At the appointed time, I undress and my eunuchs wrap me in a thick blanket. They hoist me onto their shoulders and carry me to Emperor Honghui's palace. When Honghui unwraps my face, he laughs.

"What are you doing? he asks.

"I told you. I wanted everything done properly."

He sighs and shakes his head. "I cannot believe that

something so silly is the proper way to do a thing."

"Well, it is to keep you safe," I say. "To make sure I'm not hiding any weapons in my robe. At least, that is what I have been told."

"Hmm. I wonder if something like that ever happened, that a consort or concubine tried to kill an emperor."

"It would be a very foolish thing to do," I say. "But it is you who are the emperor now. You are the person who makes the rules."

"I rather like the sound of that. Very well, from now on, the empress does not have to come to me naked. You can be dressed and come in a sedan chair."

"Are you sure?" I ask teasingly. "It could help things—" I reach out of the blanket and run a finger down the front of this yellow robe. "—progress more quickly if I arrive naked."

Honghui takes my hand and kisses the tips of my fingers. "I rather like the idea of undressing you myself."

I blush, suddenly feeling self-conscious. But also does my desire for this man—for my husband—grow. While this is not the first time we have been intimate together, it has been a long time. When I was a mere concubine, I cared not what would happen to me if the prince and I had been caught together. But as my position grew, so did the danger, and we saw each other less and less. For a brief moment, I wonder if I have even forgotten how to make love to a man of my choosing. How to truly enjoy the act and not just put on a show of pleasure for the other person's sake.

But as Honghui and I begin to kiss and touch, I remember that making love is not something someone knows how to do, but feels how to do. Our bodies come together easily, fluidly, pleasurably.

"I have another decree," Honghui says after, as we linger

naked in each other's arms.

"Hmm?" I ask, still lost in the drifting moments after lovemaking that leave your mind dizzy, as if drunk.

"When the empress comes to my bed chamber, she must stay with me until morning."

I sigh and snuggle even more tightly under his arm. "Whatever you wish, Your Majesty."

"And what is it you would wish of me, my empress?" he asks, running his fingers through my hair.

I am suddenly awake, my mind racing. Is this my moment? My chance to tell him the truth and beg his forgiveness? I lift my head to look into his face and see a man who is deliriously happy. To him, the question was nothing more than a love game. I have no desire to ruin this happiness with the truth now.

"Just...always think well of me," I say, laying my head back on his chest. "I always tried to do the right thing."

"Hmm..." He sighs, and I realize he is almost asleep. His hand slowly stops petting my chair before it falls to the mattress.

I realize that even though we have been intimate together many times, this is the first time we will sleep together. How I wish I could luxuriate in that knowledge as easily as Honghui can. Ever since I first came to the Forbidden City, this is the safest, most secure, and happiest I have been. Can I not just be happy?

Perhaps I am simply overanxious. This feeling is so very new to me, it will take time for me to get used to it. It will take time for Dongmei and Jiangfei to trust me again. Everything will simply take time. And for once, I have that time. There is no reason to rush. Everything will happen when it should.

It is time for me to learn to be content.

12

*I*s there anything more strange than choosing the women who will share your husband's bed?

I don't consider myself a jealous woman. It is normal for a family that can afford it to consist of as many concubines as possible so that a man can have many sons. But I suppose I just don't like to think about the details. Who Honghui chooses to take to his bed is not my concern. But as the empress during a consort selection, who is selected *is* my concern. It is my job to help choose young ladies who I think will please my husband, and that makes me...uncomfortable, to say the least. But I have no choice. I am the empress and must do my duty.

"I have one request," I tell him before we take our places for the selection process.

"Name it," Honghui says without hesitation.

"Yanmei," I say. "Make her a consort again, as you have with me. She is still young, and I would like to see her become a mother one day."

"It is done," he says, kissing the back of my hand. He

then waves a eunuch over. "Appoint Lady Yanmei a rank three concubine."

"Immediately, Your Majesty!" the eunuch says before shuffling off to make the announcement and shower Yanmei with gifts. I wish I could be there to see the look on her face, but the ladies who have made it through all the initial rounds of the selection process are already waiting for us in the Hall of Splendid Beauty.

Emperor Honghui takes his place in the center of the room. I sit to one side of him, and Empress-Dowager Fenfeng takes her place on the other side. Honghui and I pay her no attention. When Guozhi was emperor, he valued his mother's input in his consort selection. Honghui cares not what she thinks, so her presence is a mere formality. Once we are seated, two heavy curtains are drawn and six girls are paraded in front of us. They kowtow and then sit on their knees, their eyes downcast.

My heart races at the sight. Memories of my own selection process flood my mind and I feel nauseous. How afraid I was. How I dreaded being chosen. Even though I love Honghui, I cannot say that I am glad I was chosen that day. Had I been allowed to leave, to return to my family, I am sure I would have been able to find contentment, if not happiness, elsewhere. At least I wouldn't have been separated from my family.

I look from the corner of my eye at Honghui, and I can see that he is trying to suppress a smile. He can't help it. All these pretty young ladies are here for his pleasure. If he wanted to claim all of them for himself, he could. But he has agreed to choose no more than ten ladies, for my sake. Not because I am jealous, but because I don't think any more are necessary. I hate how wasteful the court is and would see our money put to better use. So Honghui must choose carefully.

Honghui must have felt me looking at him as he meets my gaze. He takes my hand in his reassuringly.

"What do you think, my love?" he asks me. I remember that I am supposed to be looking at the women, not him. So, I turn my eyes back to the girls—as some of them cannot be more than thirteen—and try to decide who I should pick.

But my eyes fall from their faces to their hands. They are all beautiful, naturally. They have been through many rounds of the selection process already. These girls are the most beautiful, the most elegant, the most cultured that China has to offer. If I were to choose girls based on their pretty faces, it would make no difference.

Instead, I try to discern who *wants* to be chosen. One young lady has twisted her hands in her gown so tightly, her knuckles are white. Another is shaking so hard, the flowers in her hair flutter. Another girl chews her lower lip and looks near to tears. I dismiss all these girls out of hand. Of the three who are left, I ask them their names and the names of their fathers. One girl is so nervous, she cannot even say her own name. The last two, though, speak clearly and confidently. I nod my consent to Honghui.

Honghui smiles and accepts both girls. The girls kowtow again and are led away to the inner court where they will be taken to their new lives. Another positive to choosing fewer consorts is that they are each given their own palace. And I intend to make all the ladies rank four consorts, giving them more money and privileges than if they were rank five or six. The least I can do is make their lives as comfortable as possible.

The next group of six ladies is brought in, and we go

through the same process. Honghui allows me to narrow the selection down to two or three possibilities, then he takes his choice. I breathe a sigh of relief when Fiyanggu, the chief eunuch for household affairs, tells us that the last group of ladies is about to be brought in. The process has gone smoother than I expected. The girls are brought in and I only scan their faces, as I have done all the others, but when I see the very last girl, I gasp. Had I been standing, I would have collapsed. I put my hand to my mouth to keep from crying out loud.

It's Lihua.

The *real* Lihua. The girl whose place I took at the selection process all those many months ago. Or was it years? I seem to have lost all track of time along with the rest of my senses.

"What's wrong?" Honghui asks, but I can only shake my head. For a moment, I think I must have made a mistake. It can't be Lihua...can it? How could she be here? *Why* would she be here? Why, when I sacrificed so much to take her place, would she be here now?

"N-n-nothing," I finally say. "I'm only relieved that we will soon be finished."

Honghui stretches his back and neck. "Indeed. But I have one selection left, you promised."

"Yes, of course," I say, growing more confident in my surety that the girl I saw could not have been Lihua. But when I look at the girls again, she is staring right at me! It must be her. Only Lihua would dare to look her empress in the face. And it is such a familiar face. The face that got me into all this trouble in the first place.

We are hardly identical, but the similarities are clear. Especially now, with us both dressed in our finest, we could easily be mistaken for sisters.

"Daiyu?" Honghui says, looking at me.

"Yes?" I say.

He raises his eyebrow in question. "Are you going to speak to them?"

"Oh, right," I say. I forgot that I had been sort of taking the lead by helping narrow down the selection. I go down the row, dismissing two girls easily, and then two more when they cannot tell me their names. When I get to Lihua, she answers my questions without hesitation.

"I am Liling, daughter of Huizhong, Your Majesty," she says, looking at me once again. We stare at each other for a moment. If I did not know who she was, I would assume she wanted to be chosen based on her confidence. But Lihua didn't want to be chosen when I knew her. That was *how* I knew her, because she needed someone to take her place.

Well, I suppose it was all Mingxia's doing. Mingxia found me. Mingxia bought me. Mingxia lied to me. Mingxia did whatever it took to ensure that I would take her daughter's place in the Forbidden City. Lihua on the other hand... I always did wonder how she felt about the whole thing. She had once accused me of stealing her life. Could it be that she wanted to attend the selection? She wanted a chance to be chosen? She wanted to be a consort?

She wanted to be empress.

Our eyes meet, and she nods at me so imperceptibly that I am sure no one else sees it, but in that minuscule movement, she tells me everything I need to know. She wants to be chosen.

But this is so dangerous! Is she not afraid of being caught? Is she not worried that people will ask questions? I should send her away. I can't let her ruin the life I've built here. But I think she must know what I am pondering. She hardens her gaze as a warning. If I don't ensure that she is chosen, she will expose me.

"This girl looks like you, Daiyu," Honghui says, interrupting my thoughts.

"What?" I say stupidly.

"This one—" he repeats, pointing at Lihua...or Liling, I suppose. "She looks very much like you."

I scoff a laugh. "I suppose so."

Honghui laughs with me. "I'm not sure I could handle two of you," he says, and his eyes go to the other girl, one who is more in line with the other girls he has chosen today. Girls who look nothing like me. Thinner, smaller, meeker, prettier.

Lihua shoots a look at me, commanding me to intervene. I wave to Fiyanggu. "Which of these girls has birth charts more in line with his majesty's?" I ask.

Fiyanggu quickly checks the two girls' information. "The girl Liling, Your Majesty."

"Girl?" Fenfeng asks, speaking up for the first time today. "Not lady?"

"No, your highness," Fiyanggu says. "Her father, Huizhong, is of no importance."

I see Lihua blush at this. She has impersonated a poor man's daughter just to be here. She must want to be chosen very badly, indeed.

"Still," I say, "she would be an auspicious match."

I notice Fenfeng watching me from the corner of her eye. She looks from me, to Lihua, and back to me. Surely, she cannot suspect the truth, but she must sense that *something* is going on. I have said little all morning other than to say which girls I don't want Honghui to pick. I have not encouraged him toward any particular girls until now. But I'm running out of things to say. It is clear that he prefers the other girl. If I push any more, he is bound to grow suspicious.

"Auspicious, but ugly," Fenfeng mutters loudly for all to hear.

I see Honghui's nostrils flare. "I will take Liling," he says, but from the tone in his voice, I can tell he has done it more to irritate Fenfeng than please himself. I see the other girl's shoulders slump in disappointment.

I place my hand on Honghui's arm. "Take them both, dear."

"Are you sure?" he asks me hopefully.

"Yes," I say even though in the pit of my stomach I know that this is a disaster.

Honghui cheerily motions to Fiyanggu to tell him the good news, and the other girl begins to cry joyfully.

"Thank you, Majesties!" she says as she is led away.

Lihua, though, stays and watches us, a self-satisfied grin on her face, until the curtains are drawn and Honghui, Fenfeng, and I are alone again.

"Eleven new consorts, Yanmei, and my darling empress," Honghui says thoughtfully. "Truly, I am a blessed man." He kisses me on my cheek before leaving with Fiyanggu to work out some details of the girls' appointments.

I turn to go back to the inner court where the new girls are supposed to be waiting for me to pay me respect as their empress and head of the harem, but Fenfeng's voice stops me.

"Who is that girl to you?" Fenfeng asks me.

"Who?" I ask.

She shakes her head. "Don't play stupid with me. You know her, that much is clear. But why you would pretend not to... Well, that is a puzzle, isn't it?"

"Stop trying to catch me out," I tell her. "Honghui will never listen to a word you say."

"Oh, but he does, doesn't he?" she says. "He was about to send Liling away until I spoke up."

I feel sick as I realize that she is right. Even now, when she should not have an ounce of power, her influence over the court is strong.

"Keep lying to me, dear," Fenfeng says. "It will only make the truth more sweet when I discover it." She laughs as she leaves the room and me alone with my very dark thoughts.

13

———

I had intended to do things differently as a new empress. Instead of sending the girls to their new homes, alone and confused and afraid, I wanted to make them feel welcome. Make them feel that this was their new home and their new family. But the plan has backfired, and as I am carried to my palace in a sedan chair, it is I who feel alone and confused and afraid of what will await me when I get there.

Why is Lihua here? What is her plan? What will she say to me now that she is a consort and I am the empress? Will my secret have already been exposed by the time I step out of my chair?

When I arrive, nothing seems out of sorts at first. Yanmei, Lihua, and the ten new consorts all await me in the courtyard, and they curtsey at my approach.

"Sister!" Yanmei says, trotting to me and taking my hands in hers. "Jinhai told me the news, that I am to be a consort again! Thank you! Thank you so much!"

We hug and I kiss her on both cheeks. "There is no need to thank me," I tell her. "You are my dearest friend, and it is my greatest wish that you should have a child as soon as possible."

Her eyes water as she steps back and curtseys again. "My lady is most kind and generous."

I look around at the other girls and all of them, even Lihua, are still bowing respectfully. It would appear that Lihua does not intend to draw attention to herself for the moment, which helps me breathe a little easier.

"Ladies," I say, addressing them all, "welcome home and into our family. I know that tradition would have you view me as a mother, but it is my desire that you see me more as a sister and friend. I appreciate your respect, of course, but I will not rule over you, but with you. All of us have the same goal—to keep his majesty happy and to give him as many children as possible. To that end, I hope to have no fighting or jealousy, but love and cooperation."

"Thank you, Your Majesty," all the ladies say in unison.

"In celebration of your arrival," I go on, "I would like all of you to join me for supper. Until then, please, go to your new homes, unpack, and relax. Your worries are at an end."

"May her majesty live ten thousand years!" the ladies all say. One by one, they file out of the courtyard, escorted by their new maids and eunuchs. All...but one. Lihua stays behind and we stare at each other for a moment as I wait for her to speak.

"Daiyu!" Lihua finally exclaims as she steps forward and takes me into her arms in a generous hug. I stand stone still, waiting for her to stab me in the back. She then looks at me with a pained expression. "What is wrong? Don't you remember me?"

I see Nuwa's eyes grow big at this. "Leave us," I say to all the servants. I can't have them overhearing anything that Lihua and I might have to say to each other. I then lead

Lihua to a table in the middle of the courtyard so that I can see all around us to make sure no one is eavesdropping. Even if we went into a room with closed doors, people could listen at keyholes. It is safer out in the open.

"Of course I remember you," I tell her once we are seated. "I am only confused that you are here at all. I took your place. You were free. Why would you come here? And who is Liling?"

"So many questions!" she whines. "And it has been such a long day. I'm so tired. Can we at least have some tea?"

I exhale in frustration and then wave a maid over, asking her to bring us tea and sweets. "Now," I say as soon as the treats have been delivered and I have made sure that the maid is again well away, "tell me what is going on. Why are you here? I thought you didn't want to be selected as a consort."

Lihua scoffs. "That was all the work of my mother, surely even you could figure out that much."

"I had my suspicions," I say. "But still, why would she allow you to be here now?"

"She's dead," Lihua says without any feeling.

"What?"

"The old bat gave away my life and then had the audacity to up and die. Can you believe it?"

I have to shake my head, both at the news that Mingxia is dead and at Lihua's attitude about it. She doesn't seem sad, or even very angry. More, inconvenienced.

"I'm sorry for your loss," I say politely, though I hardly feel sorry. It seems she manipulated both of us into getting what she wanted without a care for anyone else. "Why didn't you marry someone else in all this time? You could have married for love."

"Love?" she asks in almost a sneer. "You really are a

foolish peasant, aren't you? The whole point of marriage is to elevate yourself and your family. To make the best match possible. But how could I make a good match when my mother had given my identity away to someone else? I was forced to pretend to be my mother's maid, a companion. Can you believe it? It was so demeaning!"

I nod along even though I doubt Lihua ever had to do anything demeaning. She might have been called a maid, but surely she was never treated like one. She never had to cook or clean or bow and scrape.

"When Mother died, I was completely alone," she goes on more seriously, setting her teacup aside and wiping the crumbs from the side of her mouth. "I had no family and no marriage prospects. But then I heard that Emperor Honghui, may he live ten thousand years, had already selected his empress. Empress Lihua, the same woman who had been empress to Guozhi, and her new regnal name was Empress Daiyu. Well, I knew it had to be you. I don't know how you did it. When Emperor Guozhi died, I thought you would be consigned to the Temple of Grief for the rest of your life. But when I heard that you were back, that you'd been given a second chance, well, I wondered if this was my second chance as well. It has to be fate, don't you think?"

"Things certainly have worked out differently than I expected," I say cautiously. Lihua appears to be speaking honestly, respectfully, but I still have my guard up. I feel like a mouse being circled by a clever snake. If I do not keep my wits about me, she will strike. "So, you used your new identity as a maid to stand in during the new selection process."

"I followed my mother's example and used my inheritance to pay a maid to let me take her place," Lihua explains. "Then I paid a scribe to make my birth chart more in line with that of his majesty."

"I see. Well, now that you are here, what happens next?"

"What do you mean?" she asks innocently.

"You aren't going to...tell anyone what we've done, are you?" I ask. "Who we really are?"

Lihua laughs, hiding her open mouth behind her hand. "Why would I ever do that? Why, if I told everyone who you were, then I could get in trouble too, right?"

I shrug. "Things never seem to work out the way I think they will."

Lihua reaches over and places a hand on my arm. "You have nothing to fear from me, Daiyu," she says with a sweet smile. I nod and smile back, but the fact that she called me Daiyu and not Your Majesty tells me the truth. She might not intend on exposing me for the moment, but she could. I do not hesitate to think that she would reveal the truth about me if she thought it would be advantageous to her in some way.

"Well, I'm glad we had this talk," I say, standing up, indicating that it is time for her to leave. "You should visit your palace and have a rest. I'm sure it will be to your liking, much more beautiful than you are used to."

She lets out a little snort. "How can it be when I'm only a rank four concubine?" she asks me, pouting her lower lip. "Me? Such an old and dear friend. Surely you can elevate me to a higher rank. There are no rank two consorts."

She certainly wastes no time in making demands of me. What else can I do but try to keep her happy?

"Rank two is reserved for concubines and consorts who give the emperor a son," I say. "Even rank three is supposed to only be for women who have given the emperor at least a daughter."

"But Yanmei is rank three," Lihua protests.

"She has been here a long time," I say. "As long as I have.

And she is my chief lady-in-waiting. Her position was a special circumstance."

"Then make me a lady-in-waiting," Lihua says, growing irritated. Her kind demeanor is nearly gone and she looks at me with hard eyes. I don't want to give in. I don't trust her. If I give her what she wants now, the demands will continue. It won't take long for people to grow suspicious about why I have shown this girl, this man of no consequence's daughter. But what else can I do?

I smile and nod, pretending that I think her request is a splendid idea. "Of course. I will let Fiyanggu know of the change immediately."

"Oh, Daiyu!" Lihua says, hugging me and kissing me on each cheek. "Everything is going to work out beautifully, you'll see!"

I raise a hand and summon Jinhai to me. "Please inform Fiyanggu that Lady Li...umm Lady Liling—" For a moment I had forgotten what her new name was. "—has been promoted to rank-three consort and is now one of my ladies-in-waiting. Be sure that she is housed accordingly."

"Yes, of course," Jinhai says, but I see him eye me wearily, as if he suspects something is wrong. I do my best to keep my bearing, to appear confident in my decision, and Jinhai soon rushes off to find Fiyanggu. Nuwa then approaches me, and Lihua's new servants inch their way to her side.

"I'm sure it will take some time to prepare a new palace for you," I tell Lihua, trying to steer us into our proper roles as empress and concubine. "You will have to rest in your current palace until it is ready. I'm sorry for the inconvenience."

"I thank you for your kindness, my lady," Lihua says

with a deep bend of her knees and neck. "I will see you at supper."

I nod and she takes her maid's hand as she walks away, swaying perfectly on her pot-bottom shoes. She has a gracefulness that even now I do not possess.

"Are you in trouble, my lady?" Nuwa asks me, keeping her voice low.

"What?" I ask. "What do you mean?"

"I know I'm not Suyin, Your Majesty," she says. "But you can still trust me. I promise."

I laugh and slap playfully at Nuwa's arm. "Honestly, I don't know what you mean. Today is a great day for all of us. Our family has grown by leaps and bounds."

Nuwa watches me for a moment, and it is clear she is not fooled. Still, she cannot argue with me. So, she bows her head. "Yes, my lady. Of course."

I tell Nuwa that I am tired from the day's activities and wish to lie down. As soon as she is gone, I curl up on my bed and cry for the fleeting moment of peace I enjoyed as empress. How will I ever find peace now?

14

"The emperor is the kindest husband a woman could wish for!" one of the new concubines, a girl named Xiuying, says. Xiuying, Yanmei, Lihua, another concubine named Chanhui, and I are all sitting in my courtyard, embroidering warm insoles for shoes that will be distributed to the poor of Peking once winter comes. The new girls have been settled in the Forbidden City for a few weeks, and I have asked them how they are feeling about their new lives here.

"I heard you were summoned to his bed last night," Lihua says, her face looking a little sour, "for the second time."

Xiuying blushes a little. "Yes. He gifted me with this jewel." She reaches up and touches a butterfly pin in her hair. "Isn't it beautiful?"

"That is a meaningful gift," I tell her, trying to suppress a tinge of jealousy in my stomach. "His mother's name was Hudie, butterfly."

"He must really enjoy your company," Yanmei says.

Lihua snorts. "That's a kind way of putting it."

"Stop—" I try to say, but Xiuying doesn't hear me.

"Of putting what?" Xiuying asks.

"Of saying that the emperor enjoys whatever it is you do to him in bed," Lihua snaps. The maids gasp and Xiuying's face turns red as a plum.

"Enough," I say. "There is no reason to be vulgar. All of us are here for his majesty's pleasure. I am glad to see that Xiuying is performing her duties admirably."

"Thank you, Your Majesty," Xiuying says even though she is near to tears.

It is a strange situation that many concubines seem to find themselves in. Growing up, most young women, especially women from good families, are taught nothing of what happens between a man and wife in bed. They are only taught that they must obey their husband and give him sons. But most of them are completely ignorant about how babies are made. It is never spoken of between mother and daughter, must less in polite company. Even after a woman lays with her husband, it is still treated as a secret. It is something everyone does, yet no one speaks about except in the strictest of whispers, and only in reference to making babies. I had a vague idea of what men and women did in bed because I grew up so poor that I shared a room with my parents.

"Disorder is produced by women," Yanmei says, looking at Lihua as she stabs at her embroidery.

"Stop this," I say to Yanmei.

"You would let her sow jealousy among us?" Yanmei asks me plainly.

"You would let her speak to me that way?" Lihua says to me.

"Who are you?" Yanmei asks. "A fisherman's daughter? No, not even that. A fisherman has an honorable and useful trade. How was it your father was described? As a man of no consequence?"

Lihua jumps to her feet and lunges toward Yanmei. Thankfully, I was closer to Yanmei, so I am able to stand between them and hold Lihua back. The maids rush forward and hurry their ladies apart.

"Everyone leave except Lihua," I say.

"How dare you let Yanmei speak to me like that!" Lihua yells at me when everyone is gone. Though, I am never truly alone. I glance around and see Nuwa not far away. I hold my hand up to tell her to stay back.

"Lower your voice," I say to Lihua with more authority than I feel. I wonder if she knows just how afraid of her I am. Lihua scoffs and returns to her seat with her arms crossed in a huff.

"Now, what is wrong?" I ask, taking my own seat. "Why are you so hateful today?" In truth, she's been hateful nearly every day. Nothing is ever fully to her liking. Her food isn't good enough. Her silk robes are scratchy. Her eunuchs are too ugly. She complains incessantly, and the other girls have taken notice. I am afraid that it is becoming clear that I am showing Lihua favor, but no one can understand why. When I give gifts to Yanmei, everyone knows that it is because we are friends and I enjoy her company. But Lihua... Sadly, I cannot even pretend to like her, and she makes no efforts to be likable.

"How can you not know?" she asks. "The emperor has yet to summon me to his bed!"

"I'm sorry," I say. "But he has thirteen women to choose from. You are lucky that there are only thirteen. When I was a concubine for Guozhi, there were hundreds of women. When he died, most of his concubines were sent to the Temple of Grief as virgins."

"I've been here more than a month," Lihua says. "And I am a rank three consort, second only to you. There is no reason that girls of lower rank than me should be invited to the emperor's bed when I am not. You've been summoned dozens of times."

I bite my tongue to keep from informing her that she is not second to me. Yanmei is second to me. And since Honghui has already shown favor to some of the other girls, Lihua truly has no rank among the ladies of our small harem no matter what her title may be. But I don't tell her this. For one thing, she should already know. She's not stupid, and she understands social order better than I ever have. Secondly, it will only make her more angry if I point it out to her. She's never been one to accept hard truths.

"I'm sorry that the emperor has not summoned you," I say. "But the department of household affairs sets the emperor's schedule for…evening activities. Have you spoken to your eunuch?"

"He wants me to pay a bribe for just the chance of being selected," Lihua moans. "Nearly my entire monthly allowance!"

I have to nod knowingly. I remember when I was a concubine I was told the same thing, that in order to be chosen, I would have to bribe certain members of the department of household affairs to encourage the emperor to select me. I never paid the bribe because I didn't want to be selected. I didn't want to stand out. I didn't want to be noticed. Still, I inadvertently drew the emperor's attention in other ways and quickly climbed the ranks until I was second only to the empress and then took her place when she died in childbirth.

"That is one way women get the emperor's attention," I

say. "Though, I never did that. I found other ways to get his attention."

"Am I supposed to find a way to save your life?" Lihua asks. "Is it not enough that I am the whole reason you are here at all?"

"Shh!" I say, stepping closer to her. "Stop talking about that. You are going to get us found out."

"It's true, though," she says, stomping her foot. "You stole my life. You owe me."

"I didn't steal anything!" I say, finally losing control of myself. "I didn't want to be here. I didn't want to be chosen. Your mother lied to me and trapped me here. She knew I was likely to be chosen based on your stupid birth chart. I didn't steal your life—I was tricked into it. If anything, your mother stole my life from me! I'm not supposed to be here."

Lihua lets out a confused chuckle. "What? Do you actually want to live in the dirt on the streets where we found you? I remember that filthy, stinking hovel your family lived in. My mother made you an empress. Are you truly that ungrateful?"

I sigh and shake my head. "It's more complicated than that. I love Emperor Honghui and Emperor Guozhi's daughters. I know that I'm infinitely blessed to live this life. But I miss my family. It hurts so much that I don't know what happened to them."

"I'm sure they're fine," Lihua says. "Mama paid them enough for you. They must be living well somewhere."

"You don't know where they are?" I ask. "What happened to them?" I've been wanting to ask her about them for some time, but I wasn't sure how to broach the topic.

"No. Why would I? They don't mean anything to me."

"After I was selected as a consort, your mother was

supposed to give them more money. Do you know if she ever did?"

Lihua shrugs. "I know she went to see them, but I don't know if she ever found them. I didn't ask."

My heart sinks in disappointment. With Mingxia dead, I don't know that I'll ever be able to find my family now. Who else would know what happened to them?

"It looks like we are both stuck here," Lihua says, and her tone is kinder than I think I've ever heard her speak. "But maybe we can find a way to make the best of it."

"What do you mean?" I ask.

"We can help each other," she says. "Speak to Honghui. Encourage him to take me to his bed."

I remember when I once spoke to Guozhi about such matters. I tried to encourage him to take the Lady An, Dongmei's mother, to his bed. For reasons I never quite understood, he became enraged at me. Said I was overstepping my bounds and that I was not to speak of such matters with him again. It was our first fight, and it nearly ruined our relationship. I don't think that Honghui would react similarly, but he also did not want to select Lihua at all. He might not appreciate me pushing a girl he doesn't want into his bed. Still, I suppose I can at least mention Lihua to him. After all, he only has thirteen women. He can spend at least one night with her and make her a proper wife. Give her at least a chance of becoming pregnant.

"I will see what I can do," I say.

Lihua smiles and hugs me. "Oh, thank you, Daiyu. You aren't going to regret it, I promise!"

"But what are you going to do for me?" I ask her, taking a chance.

"What?" she asks.

"You said we could help each other, right? What can you do for me?"

Her smile falters. After all, she has no standing within the court. She has nothing to offer me.

"Well, I'll continue to keep your secret, of course," she says.

I give her a tight smile and nod. "Of course."

And with that, it is clear between us that Lihua has no intention of helping me or being friends. She wants to rise in power in the inner court. She wants a son. And she will leverage all her power over me to get it.

I will never be able to trust her.

15

"I'm pregnant."

Honghui stares at me for a moment, as if he does not understand the words I just said. Then, a smile slowly crosses his face and he drops to his knees in front of me. He wraps his arms around my hips and kisses my stomach.

"May my son be born strong and healthy," he says on a sigh. I can't help but chuckle at him. He stands back up and pushes my hair from my face as he kisses my lips.

"How far along are you?" he asks.

"About two months," I say. "After I missed my first courses, Nuwa and I decided to wait one more month to make sure it was not a fluke. But since I have missed them again, we think there is only one explanation."

"I can't believe you waited so long to tell me," he says, slightly wounded.

"You have enough things to worry about," I say. "I didn't want to get your hopes up if it wasn't true."

"You never have to shoulder any burden alone," he says.

If only you knew, I thought to myself. "Well, you know now," I tell him.

"Does anyone else know?" he asks. "You mentioned your maid."

"Yes, Nuwa knows," I say. "And Yanmei. But they are sworn to secrecy until I am ready to tell the others. The other ladies are sure to be jealous."

"Do the new ladies not get along? Do they not like you?"

"It's not that," I say. "They seem mostly content. But all of them crave a child of their own. They already see me as the most privileged of the lot, the one with the most money and freedom and time with you. For me to also be the first to give birth, some of them will have no choice but to feel at least a bit jealousy."

Honghui nods and sinks down onto the bed with a bit of worry on his face. "Well, you realize that after tonight, I won't be able to summon you to my bed chamber again until after you give birth."

My eyes water. I knew this was coming, but to hear it said out loud hurts my soul. "I know."

Honghui takes my hand and pulls me to sit beside him. "This is the reason why I have concubines, after all. While you are pregnant, I must spread my essence and try to have as many children as possible."

I can't help but chuckle at his words.

"What?" he asks.

"'Spread your essence,'" I repeat. "It makes everything sound very official, doesn't it?"

He laughs with me. "I know. I'm not sure it all really works that way. After all, Guozhi had hundreds of women and only two daughters to show for it. I have known men with only one wife who had half a dozen sons."

"I know," I say, nodding. "My father—" I have to catch

myself. I was about to say that my father only had one wife and five living children, but I stop myself in time to remember that Honghui still thinks that my father was a great Manchu general who died with only one daughter to his great name. "My father's brother," I correct, "he had only one wife but five children. I'm sure my mother would have had many children had Father not died so young."

"Well, as soon as you are able," Honghui says, kissing me again, "we will have another child, I'm sure of it. As many as your heart desires."

"Let's just worry about this one for now," I say, touching my still-flat stomach. I can hardly believe that there is a baby growing inside of me. The mere thought of it makes my heart flutter.

"My son," Honghui says, placing his hand on mine.

His words suddenly make me feel a bit anxious. My parents only ever had daughters. Guozhi had daughters. What if I do not give Honghui the son he, and the dynasty, so desperately needs? But it is considered treason to even think such things. To speak of an emperor's unborn child as anything but a strong and healthy male is the same as cursing the child to be female.

"I know what you are thinking," Honghui says, interrupting my thoughts.

"Hmm?" I ask.

"You are worried that the child might be a daughter," he says.

I want to tell him he is wrong, that I would never think such a thing. But somehow, despite everything I have hidden from this man, he knows me better than anyone.

"It will be a boy," I say dutifully. "But...if it is a girl, will you be angry?"

"No!" he says without hesitation. "How could I be disappointed with a little Daiyu? I love you, and I will love all our children, boys and girls. Besides, I already—"

He pauses for a moment and my eyes shoot to his face. His cheeks quickly blush red for only a moment before he smiles again.

"Already what?" I ask.

"I already love this child, no matter what."

As someone who has spent years living each moment of my life in a lie, I know he is not telling the whole truth. The part about loving me and loving this child, even if it is a girl, I believe is true. I suppose I cannot accuse him of lying, but he nearly said something that he did not mean to say. But since I also almost spoke of things I meant to keep secret only mere moments ago, I suppose I cannot fault him for having some secrets of his own. As long as he loves me and this baby, I shall have to be content with that.

"There is something else I need to speak with you about," I say. "You mentioned that you will have to summon the other ladies to your bed chamber while I am with child."

"We should meet secretly," he says.

"What?"

"Like we used to," he says. "Remember?"

I blush. How could I forget? "Oh?"

"Officially, I am not allowed to summon you to me," he says. "But after I have...performed my husbandly duty with the others, I could sneak out of my room and meet you."

"I'd like that," I say. "But, as I was saying, it's been brought to my attention that you have not yet summoned Liling. That she is still a maiden."

Honghui leans back and is no longer smiling. I feel a rush of panic, of fear that I have made him angry or am treading on dangerous ground.

"Of course, you know what is best," I say quickly. "And I only want you to be happy."

"What are you blabbering?" he asks. "Speak plainly. I don't need false flattery, not from you."

"Yes, of course," I say, trying to calm myself. This is Honghui, not Guozhi. He might not always like what I have to say, but he will not punish me for doing my job, for caring for the women of the inner court. "I have reviewed the records with Fiyanggu, and you have summoned all of the ladies at least once except for Liling. She has expressed her unhappiness to me. I know that who you summon is between you and Fiyanggu, but as your wife, I am encouraging you to pay attention to Lady Liling. It is your duty to her."

He sighs. "You are right, naturally. I just..." He shrugs.

"What is wrong?" I ask. "Does she not please you?"

"Of course she does," he says. "She looks like you. How could she not please me?"

"Then, why don't you want her?" I ask.

"It's *because* she looks like you," he says. "I suppose it is hard to explain. I know that love is a poor basis for a marriage. That duty and honor should come first. But I do love you, Daiyu. I summon you here so often because I love you and value your company and counsel. According to Fiyanggu, an emperor only needs to summon his empress once per month. But if I only saw you once a month, I would die. My heart and my...my manhood would shrivel into nothing."

"And I love you," I say, squeezing his hand. "But what does that have to do with Lady Liling? You summon the other ladies."

"They don't look like you," he says. "Surely you noticed."

"I did," I say. "I thought that, maybe, it was because you

preferred them. That you might love me, but you don't find me attractive."

"You are a silly woman," he says. "It's because I don't want to think about you when I perform my duties with them. If I think about you while I have another woman in my bed, it makes me feel...as if I am dishonoring you somehow."

"Oh," I say. "I see." And I do, to an extent. I suppose I never thought about things from a man's perspective. Women only exist for their pleasure, after all. When I was with Honghui while Guozhi was still alive, I did feel a bit guilty. But I never imagined that men might feel such guilt as well. After all, it is expected for men to have as many concubines as possible. It is not infidelity, but for the good of the family. For an emperor, it is for the good of the nation.

"Why did you push me to select her?" Honghui asks me. "You must know that I would not have done so if you did not want it."

"I thought you picked her in order to anger Fenfeng," I say teasingly.

He chuckles. "Well, there was that. But it was clear you were steering me toward her before Fenfeng spoke up."

I shrug. "I don't know. Maybe it is because we look so similar. She wants so much to please you. Perhaps if I help her, I will be helping myself in some strange way."

"Well, no matter the reasons, I did select her and she is my concubine. It is my responsibility to help her fulfill her duty of becoming pregnant."

"Thank you," I say. "I know it will make her happy, and that will make life in the inner court easier for all of us."

"Hmm. Is she a difficult girl?" he asks.

"I think that anyone who is unhappy can make those around them miserable. I try not to blame her."

"Don't let her bully you," Honghui says. "You are the empress. She's no one. I could even send her to the Temple of Grief if she were to act badly."

"No!" I say, fearing the havoc she would cause in my life if she were to be dismissed so coldly. "No, please, nothing so dramatic. I'm sure that after you have summoned her to your bed chamber a few times, she will be content."

"Now I have to summon her a few times?" he whines.

I take a pillow and throw it at him. He bats it away and tosses another one back at me. We playfully slap at each other and toss pillows before he catches my wrist and pulls me to him, tickling me and making me laugh until I cry. He then pins my arms down and kisses me, careful not to put all of his weight on top of me.

"Thank you, Daiyu," he says between kisses.

"For what?" I ask, my eyes growing heavy.

"For being the perfect empress, and soon, the perfect mother."

I let out a long sigh as she kisses down my body, paying close attention to my stomach. Lihua certainly still poses a problem for me. She is dangerous. But if I give Honghui a son, he will surely go to the end of the earth to protect me and keep me safe. Soon, the dangers will all pass. I'm sure of it.

16

"**A**re you really having a baby?" Dongmei asks me, poking at my still flat stomach. I'm now about three months along and still find it hard to believe. I don't feel very different. I certainly don't look any different. If it weren't for the lack of my monthly bleed, I wouldn't know I was pregnant.

"I guess so," I say with a shrug. "If Heaven is willing."

Jiangfei just watches me with big, worried eyes. I know what she is thinking, what she has been thinking ever since I first told the girls that I was with child. She is afraid I am going to die. And yet, I have said nothing to calm her fears. How can I? Her mother, Empress Caihong, died in childbirth. My own dear mother nearly died from a miscarriage. It is a tragedy that only women face, and a fear only we can understand. It happens far too often. I cannot promise Jiangfei that I won't die, so what can I say to her? I have been as kind and loving as possible, but I cannot take away the very real fear she has of me dying and leaving her once again. Wouldn't that just be the way of things? For me to finally be safe and secure in my life and home and still be dragged away by the gods?

Lihua brings a tray of tea to our table and passes the cups around. She has been far quieter, more content, and—dare I say—more pleasant since Honghui invited her to his bed chamber. He has only done so twice. He has invited some of the other girls, such as Yanmei, more often, but Lihua has not complained. There has been a peace in the inner court I have not experienced before. I had doubted that a home with so many concubines for one man could ever be happy, but perhaps I had been wrong.

"The dowager empress approaches!" a eunuch announces. I cannot hide a groan as I stand to greet my "guest." Though, I am curious as to why she would call on me. Other than for morning greetings, I have hardly spoken to her. I do not visit her palace, and she does not call upon me. So this is a strange occurrence.

Fenfeng enters the palace in full regalia, her finest gown, her tallest headdress, the total of her household trailing behind her. I am not sure if she means to intimidate me or honor me. The fact that she did not announce her visit makes me think intimidation is her intention. She did not give me the opportunity to prepare myself or my home for her arrival. But I have no reason to be afraid of her, so I suppress any insecurity I feel as deep and low in my stomach as possible.

"Your Majesty," the dowager empress says as she kneels before me. I give her a polite bow back.

"Mother," I say. "To what do I owe this visit?"

"I wanted to congratulate you on your pregnancy," she says. "And I have brought gifts." She motions to a servant who brings forth an adorable pair of embroidered tiger shoes fit for a prince on a red pillow. Another servant then brings a pillow piled high with gold and jade jewelry.

"Thank you, Mother," I say. "This was unnecessary, but I thank you all the same. I am sure my son will look beautiful in such decorations."

"I know I already congratulated you privately," she says, and she had. After I told Honghui the happy news, the pregnancy was announced throughout the Forbidden City, and the next morning during greetings, Fenfeng expressed her joy at the news, and I accepted her congratulations graciously. She would, technically, be the baby's grandmother, after all. Though I have no plans to ever let the woman anywhere near my baby. I wish I could keep her away from Jiangfei and Dongmei completely, but, unfortunately, the girls are somewhat fond of their grandmother. While I have come and gone from their lives over and over again, Fenfeng has been a constant, steady presence.

"But I wanted to publicly declare my love for you and the prince you carry," Fenfeng goes on. "The future of the Qing Dynasty rests within you."

I instinctively wrap my arms around my stomach. Her words, and even her tone, seem kind and genuine. And yet, there is something in her words that set me on edge. That sound a warning in the back of my mind. Of course, if I were to say anything or reject her words, I would look paranoid. So, I can do nothing but bow my head and thank her for her gifts.

"Your words are appreciated and noted," I say. There is an awkward silence. I have nothing more to say to her and am unsure as to why she came at all. She says it was to make her congratulations public, but it was hardly necessary.

"I also wanted to inform you that I am in need of a new lady-in-waiting," she finally says. "One of my girls has decided to abandon me to get married, the selfish thing. I thought it best to choose a new one from among my son's wives so as to ensure that she will never leave me."

I can feel the ladies, the concubines, around me shift on their feet and mutter to one another under their breath. But as they are all behind me, I cannot see their expressions. I don't know which girls would see this opportunity as an honor or a punishment. While I have insisted that the court be more frugal, my monetary policies do not apply to the dowager empress, and she still has a huge allowance that she uses to pay her servants, including her ladies, generously. But she is also known to be an exacting mistress, expecting nothing less than perfection from those who serve her. While Guozhi was still alive, I am sure there were more benefits to serving her, as she had the emperor's ear. But now that Honghui is emperor, I am not sure serving the dowager empress would raise any girl in his estimation. But if Fenfeng wants a servant from among the ladies, there is nothing I can do about it. I cannot deny her.

My first thought is that she has come to claim Yanmei. It is well-known that Yanmei is not only my lady, but my dear friend. If Fenfeng was to take Yanmei from me, I am not sure what I would do. I would have to deny her, which would make me look like an unfilial daughter and could hurt my reputation, as the story would certainly spread beyond the inner court, and perhaps even beyond the red walls of the Forbidden City.

"The Lady Liling has made a very favorable impression on me," Fenfeng says. "It is she I would like to take into my own household."

A warning rattles around in my head so loudly, I have to put my hands to my ears to block out the noise. But it does no good as the sound is coming from inside. Liling? She means Lihua. Fenfeng wants Lihua? I think back to the conversation Fenfeng and I had after the consort selection. She knew that there was something going on between me and Lihua. She didn't know what, but Lihua and I clearly knew each other, yet we pretended that we didn't. Does Fenfeng know the truth about us? Surely not. If she did, she would have done something about it already. A Han Chinese among the emperor's concubines? A Han Chinese empress? If such a thing were to be discovered, I would be arrested immediately, and Honghui would not be able to save me.

No, Fenfeng does not know—yet. Perhaps she hopes to pull Lihua into her confidence. To lure the truth out of her.

"My lady!" Lihua says, dropping to her knees. "This is such an honor! I cannot believe you have ever taken notice of me, much less thought favorably of me."

My mouth goes dry. Lihua must know that the dangers around us are a hundredfold if we are separated. If we cannot confer with one another and each know what the other is doing. Of course she does. Lihua is not stupid. She is, in fact, far smarter than I am. Could she have planned this? Has she already been speaking with Fenfeng and I didn't know? It is possible, I suppose. I can hardly watch everything that is going on in a home as large as this.

Everyone is looking at me, waiting for me to consent to Fenfeng's "request." It is only a request in formality. Normally, I would never imagine denying such a request from my mother-in-law. Whatever she desires, it is my job to supply. And while I would be willing to risk denying her if she had requested Yanmei, I am not sure I can do so for Lihua. Everyone knows that Yanmei is like a sister to me, and for Fenfeng to try and take her away would be seen a spiteful. Such a disagreement between a woman and her mother-in-law would make us both look bad. But Lihua... If I were to fight Fenfeng for her, it would arouse even more suspicion. I have made Lihua one of my own ladies-in-waiting, but it must be clear to all those around us that we are not particularly close. People still seem confused as to why I pushed to have her selected as a concubine in the first place. If I were to deny Fenfeng this seemingly small request, far too many people would then want to know why. And I do not want anyone digging into my past to try and find some connection between us.

"Of course," I say, forcing a sweet smile. "What an honor for dear Liling."

"Thank you, Your Majesty," Lihua says, giving me a bow before going to stand behind Fenfeng.

"I'll see you again soon, my dear," Fenfeng says to me as she turns to leave. "I want to make sure that the mother of my grandson is having only the best care."

"My ladies and maids are doing an excellent job of taking care of me," I say. "I'll employ a midwife of my own choosing when the time for the birth grows nearer."

"Of course," Fenfeng says with a bow. "Good day, Your Majesty."

"Good day, Mother," I say, glad to see the back of her.

Everyone, from ladies to maids to Jiangfei and Dongmei, let out sighs of relief as Fenfeng leaves my courtyard. I think everyone expected the conversation to go much more worse than it had.

"Good riddance," Yanmei mutters in my ear, and I know she is referring to Lihua no longer being part of our household. Indeed, I wish I could relish in being free of her. But I cannot help but feel that there is something far more sinister at play in what just happened.

17

———

An autumn storm rages outside my palace. It has been raining for days, soaking the ground and keeping all of us trapped inside. But instead of the weather gradually getting better, it seems to only be getting worse. It is nearing nighttime, but it is as if the sun never rose today. I can only count the time by the bells that are struck by eunuchs each hour. I am sitting silently near a brazier with Yanmei and a couple of other ladies nearby. It is too dark to do embroidery or paint. One of the girls, though, is skilled on the erhu, so even in the dark, she can play beautifully. The somber tunes that drift from the instrument to our ears are suitable to the dark and melancholy weather. And they match my mood as well.

I am nearly four months pregnant, but I'm starting to think that something is wrong. I have no gained weight, nor do I have any of the other supposed signs of pregnancy. No nausea, no tiredness. I do not feel as if a prince is growing in my belly, or even a princess for that matter. Everyone is flitting around me, making me comfortable, treating me as if I am a delicate vase that might break. I play along because I know that helping prepare for a baby's birth brings them joy. Indeed, I have enjoyed embroidering little shirts and pants, thinking about where the baby will sleep, and imagining how much my life will change when there is a little one to take care of. I think that having this baby might help fill the gaping hole in my heart where my sisters used to be. For the younger ones, Junli and Huanji, I was almost like a second mother to them. I have done my best to be a mother to Jiangfei and Dongmei, but I have made so many mistakes, been away from them so often, they have had a difficult time accepting me as their mother. Jiangfei seems to be slowly learning to trust me again, but Dongmei… I don't know. I can only hope things will get better with time.

But a new baby, one of my own, one I can raise from birth, is a new chance for me to have a family again. Of course, Honghui is my husband, and Yanmei is as a sister to me. But a baby, even a girl, would help bind us together in a very real and permanent way. I truly believe that a baby will give me the security I haven't felt since I first left my family's home. I do not believe that even Lihua could undermine me if I give Honghui the child he so desperately needs.

"Enough," I say, and the girl playing the erhu stops immediately. "I'm sorry, but I'm tired. Please leave me."

"Of course, Your Majesty," the ladies say as they stand and bow their way out of the room.

"Yanmei, you may stay," I say.

"Certainly," she says. "I hardly want to try and make it back to my palace in this downpour."

I feel sort of bad for sending the other girls away. They will certainly be soaked before they even reach the edge of my courtyard, much less back to their own palaces. But I need to be alone.

"Are you feeling all right, Your Majesty?" Nuwa asks me. "Can I fetch you anything? Or even a doctor, perhaps?"

"I'm fine," I tell her. "Just...unsettled."

She nods knowingly. She too has noticed my lack of pregnancy symptoms. She tries to tell me that everything is fine. That some women don't even know they are pregnant before going into labor. I'm not sure I believe that, though. I saw my mother through enough pregnancies to know the signs and what to expect. I can't tell Nuwa that, though, so I have to pretend to rely on her expertise.

"Why don't you go have your supper," I tell Nuwa. "I'll be fine with Yanmei."

"Of course, my lady," Nuwa says, bowing her way out of the room and closing the door behind her.

"Are you really all right?" Yanmei asks me.

"Why do you ask?"

"You just seem to be carrying a very heavy burden on your mind," she says. I feel a pain pluck at my heart and I have to turn away, stare out the window at the rain as it pools in the courtyard.

"I've been thinking about Empress Caihong a lot lately," I say.

Yanmei nods and sits on a nearby chair. "I understand. She was the last empress to be pregnant, after all."

"Before she died, she had a dream, a nightmare. One in which she saw herself and her baby. They were robed in white."

Yanmei sucks in a breath. "Dear me."

I nod. "I tried to tell her not to worry. That it was just a dream and there was no meaning in it. That she was only feeling guilty over what happened to Lady An. But she believed it was a message from the gods, a warning. She thought that the gods were going to demand her life and the life of her child for her sins."

"That poor woman," Yanmei says, wiping a tear from her cheek. "She was a good empress, a kind lady. She didn't deserve what happened to her. She had nothing to do with Lady An's fate."

"I know," I say. "And that is what I told her. And I believed it...up until the moment she died."

"Oh...Daiyu," Yanmei says.

"As she died, her thoughts were of Lady An. She didn't say as much, but I think she thought the dream had come true. At least she died thinking the baby had lived. If she had known that the baby had died as well..." I shudder. "I am sure her spirit would never be able to rest."

"Hopefully they are together, wherever they are," Yanmei says.

The sky lights up for a moment with a flash, revealing only dark clouds overhead as far as the eye can see. The thunder that follows is gentle and rolling, as if from far away. I have a feeling the storm is still going to linger for some time. I run my hands over my flat stomach.

"Do you think there is any truth in it, though?" I ask. "That the gods might punish us and our unborn children for our past sins?"

"No," Yanmei says, but there is no conviction in her voice. If I were not pregnant, I think she would have given a different answer. As it is, though, she is wanting to comfort me. And, of course, she doesn't want to say anything negative lest she accidentally lay a curse on me and the baby. "You've done nothing wrong."

I have to laugh at that. Yanmei has no idea the terrible things I've done. I cannot even say that my intentions were always good. When I slept with Honghui while Guozhi was still alive, I cared not that Guozhi would be hurt by my actions. Had I become pregnant, I would have let Guozhi think the baby was his and raise it as his own. Suyin died in my place. I did not speak up for Lady An even though I knew she was innocent.

I wonder for a moment about Empress Caihong. I liked her and thought she was a good woman. But is it possible that she held a world of dark secrets hidden within her heart? I suppose it's possible. If the gods did enact some sort of horrible revenge on her, it could have been because of something else entirely unrelated to Lady An's death. And if the gods killed her and her baby, could they not also do the same to me?

"Yanmei," I say, doing my best to choke back tears, "you don't know me. You don't know what I've done."

"Shh!" Yanmei says, rushing over to me. "Whatever it is, do not speak so loudly."

"What?" I ask as she tries to wipe the tears from my cheeks.

"You never know who might be listening," she says, glancing at the door. Of course, she is right. I lower my voice.

"I have to tell you the truth," I say. "It's eating me up inside."

Yanmei shakes her head. "You don't need to tell me."

"Do...do you know?" I ask. I don't know how it could be possible, but I suppose Yanmei might have learned the truth about me somehow.

"No," she says, shaking her head. "At least, not specifically. But I know you have secrets. I know that you...are not quite who you claim to be."

"Just tell me," I say. "What do you know? *How* do you know?"

"I don't know," she says. "It is just clear to me that you are not from a wealthy family. You are too...innocent."

I chuckle at that. "Is that your kind way of calling me stupid?"

"No," she says. "I would never say you are stupid. Stupid people cannot learn. But you always seemed very...ignorant of certain things. And it was clear that you never wanted to be here before. I was shocked when you agreed to marry Honghui. I thought you hated it here."

"I did," I say. "You were right about that. But Honghui and I... Well..."

"It is more than a political marriage, isn't it?" Yanmei says. I can only nod. "Well, he did save your life. I can see why you would easily fall in love with him."

I wish I could tell her more of the story. Tell her how we fell in love long before that. That the reason he saved my life was because he was already in love with me. But if I tell her any more, she would surely be upset with me.

"At least you are happy now, right?" she says.

"Yes," I say. "Yes, I am happy. I think I could continue to be happy. But, oh, Yanmei, I've done something so terrible—"

"Does Liling know what it is?" Yanmei asks.

"Y-yes," I say, surprised by how easily Yanmei is putting everything together. But I suppose I should not be so surprised. Yanmei has always been quite clever.

"Well, that explains a lot," she says with a frustrated sigh. "She's blackmailing you, isn't she?"

"Sort of," I say. "She and I, we are in this together. If she were to tell...what she knows about me, it would ruin her as well. But she is so devious, I have no doubt that she would fall on her own sword if it meant I would follow her."

"I don't know," Yanmei says. "Granted, I don't know Liling very well. Certainly not as well as you do. But she seems like a very selfish person to me. If what you say is true, then you have more power than you give yourself credit for. Liling will not risk the life she has here. Why, if she were to give Honghui a son, she could be made a rank-two consort! She could be the mother of the next emperor. No, she won't risk that just to hurt you."

I let out a brief sigh of relief. "Do you really think so?"

"I am certain," she says with a smile. She takes my hand in hers and leads me to my bed chamber, ushering me to my bed. "Now, just rest, Your Majesty. You are under a lot of pressure and need to relax."

"But, Yanmei," I say, holding tightly to her hand so she can't leave me. "I really feel that I need to tell you—"

"Shh!" Yanmei says, putting a finger to my lips. "Sleep on it. I can see that it is worrying you. I wish you wouldn't tell me. The more people who know...whatever it is, the greater risk to yourself. But you seem near to bursting. Try to sleep first. Tomorrow, if you still need to tell me, I will listen, okay?"

I nod. "Okay." I wish I could tell her now, get it over with. But there is wisdom in what she says. I am near to bursting. If I pour out my soul to her now, I may regret it in the morning. I already feel better for having talked to her. I'm sure she is right about Lihua putting her own well-being ahead of hurting me. Perhaps if I sleep soundly in this knowledge, I won't feel such a strong need to tell her the whole truth when I wake up.

Yanmei leaves me and I do my best to sleep. The rain and thunder grow louder, and then softer again, and I toss and turn. Sometimes I feel light as a feather, other times I feel the weight of a stone on my stomach. I'm drifting, somewhere very near sleep but not quite there, when I feel a sharp pain deep inside. I cry out as I sit up and throw back the covers. I pull up my sleeping gown and cry out when I see it.

Blood...so much blood.

18

The midwife's face is grim as she speaks in low tones to Nuwa. Yanmei sits next to me, her arm around my shoulder.

"What's wrong?" I demand. "What happened to my baby?"

When I saw the blood, I panicked. I screamed. I thought I was going to die just like Empress Caihong did. Nuwa immediately sent for a midwife while she and Yanmei did their best to calm me down.

"Your Majesty," the midwife, a middle-aged woman I have never met before, sits on the bed, facing me, and pats my hand. "There never was any baby."

"What?" I ask, confused. "What do you mean?"

"Your maid tells me that you never had any signs of being pregnant other than the lack of your monthly bleed, is that correct?"

"Umm...yes," I say. "But Nuwa told me that not all women have symptoms. That it was normal."

"Yes," the midwife says. "It can be. But pregnancy is far more complicated than many people realize."

I rub my temple. "What are you saying?"

"I don't believe you were ever pregnant," the midwife says.

"Then why am I bleeding?" I ask. "Am I not having a miscarriage?"

"Your monthly has merely returned," she says. "It appears a little heavier than normal, considering the months that were missed. But you were never with child, Your Majesty. I'm sorry."

I feel as if the breath has been knocked out of me, as if something has been taken from me, something very precious. My child. My own dear wanted—needed—child is gone. And this horrible woman is saying that there never was any baby to begin with.

Part of me believes her, knows that she is right. But by the same token, she must be horribly wrong.

"No," I say. "No, I don't believe you. Why would I suddenly miss my monthly for so long? One month, yes, maybe. That is why we waited to tell his majesty—" My voice catches in my throat. Honghui. He is going to be so disappointed. Tears fill my eyes, and if I keep talking, I fear they will break free.

"Things such as this sometimes happen," the midwife explains to me. "During times of great stress. Or have you started eating or drinking something new? Some foods or teas can cause a woman's monthly to stop."

"You have been very stressed ever since...*she* arrived," Yanmei whispers to me.

"I'm *always* under stress," I snap at her. "You don't know my life!"

Yanmei leans back as if I might bite her and her eyes go big. She's clearly hurt by my words, and I regret that, but if a little stress was enough to stop my monthly bleed, then I should have stopped having it a long time ago. No, that can't be what happened. I had to have been pregnant.

"I'm sorry," I force out. "But you must be wrong," I say to the midwife. "I must have been pregnant. Or there must be something else wrong with me."

"I checked the blood," the midwife says. "There is no... no sign of a baby. And it is not still trapped inside. There is nothing in your uterus other than a bit of blood, and that will pass over the next few days, I'm sure of it."

"Then get out!" I yell. "You are useless to me!"

"Yes, of course, Your Majesty," the woman says as she stands and bows her way out of the room.

"Shall I send for someone else?" Nuwa asks me as she nervously twists a handkerchief in her hands. "A physician perhaps? Or a different midwife?"

"No," I say, my anger subsiding and giving way to grief. The tears I had been holding back start to fall down my cheeks as I come to terms with the fact that the midwife was right. I was never pregnant. I've seen miscarriages before. I know how bloody and painful and dangerous they are. Other than a little mild cramping that is typical for my monthly bleed, I feel nothing abnormal.

Yanmei puts her arms around me and hugs me tightly. "I'm so sorry, Daiyu. I know how important this baby was to you, to all of us."

"How?" I manage to choke out. "How did this happen? I was so sure...so sure..."

She nods, her eyes glassy. I'm not the only person who lost the baby, but the entire court did. I look to Nuwa and see that she is wiping tears from her own cheeks. I reach out to her and summon her to my bedside. She collapses to the floor.

"I'm so sorry, Your Majesty," she says. "I'm so stupid! This is all my fault. I should have known better."

"No," I say. "You were in earnest. You had no reason to think I wasn't pregnant."

"I shouldn't have ignored the signs," she says. "I mean, the lack of them. I should have realized—"

"Stop this," I say. "None of us could have known. We were simply mistaken."

There is a knock on the door and another maid sticks her head into the room. "My lady, Emperor Honghui is here. He heard that a midwife was summoned and is concerned for your well-being."

I let out a heavy sigh. He's going to be so disappointed with me. But there is nothing I can do to make the situation better.

"Send him in," I say. I then dismiss Nuwa and Yanmei. I don't wish to have an audience for such a personal conversation.

Honghui rushes into the room and sits on the bed, facing me. He takes my hand and kisses my cheeks.

"My darling," he says, looking me over. He then looks at my stomach, but he seems afraid to touch it. "What's happened. Did you lose the baby? I'm so sorry!"

"No," I say stupidly. I wish I'd had time to think of a better way to tell him what has happened.

"So, the baby is all right?" he says, and I see relief flood over his face.

"No," I say. "No. There...there never was any baby. I was never pregnant."

"What?" he asks, sitting back, almost pulling away from me. "What do you mean you were never pregnant?"

"Just that," I say. "I-I-I misread the signs. I made a mistake. I'm sorry."

He lets go of my hand and turns away, resting his elbows on his knees, rubbing his face. "You made a mistake? How? How is such a thing possible?"

"My monthly had stopped," I try to explain. I reach out and lightly touch his shoulder. "And that usually means that there is a baby on the way. But I never had any of the other signs."

"Other signs?" he asks. He stands up and walks away, beyond my reach from my place in the bed where I lay like a sick woman. "So you should have known, then."

"I...I guess so," I say.

"You have the best maids," Honghui says. "Access to the best midwives. You should have known. Should have made certain before telling me. What am I to tell the rest of the court?"

His words hurt like a knife in my chest. "That's what you are worried about?" I can hardly believe what I am hearing. "You are worried about what to tell your advisors and counselors? What about me? What about our—" My words catch as I start to sob again.

"Our what?" Honghui asks. "Our son? There never was a son. You lied to me."

"I didn't lie to you!" I say. "I made a mistake. I would never—" I want to say that I would never lie to him, but that in itself would be a lie. Our whole marriage is based on a lie. All I have ever done is lie to him. But that is the only lie I have told. Everything else I have ever told him has been the truth. Other than the first lie, my great secret, I would never lie to him, never deceive him.

"You know me," I say, trying to calm myself down. "You know how much I wanted this child. It was a mistake. An honest mistake, I swear to you."

He shakes his head and looks away from me for a

moment. He seems calmer when he faces me again. "I...I believe you."

"You do?" I ask hopefully. In truth, I'm not so sure. There is something in his tone that I can't quite interpret.

"Yes," he says. "But you must understand, I am worried about how the rest of the court will react. There are still people out there who think I should not be emperor. Who think that you should not be empress. A child—a son— would have legitimized everything."

"I'm sorry," I say. "I did not realize that we were still in a precarious position."

"It's not a serious threat," he says. "I'm not going to be deposed. There isn't really anyone to take my place. But some people at court just do all that they can to undermine me, to make things difficult for me. A child would put everyone in their place."

"A child could still come," I say. "We can keep trying."

"Yes," he says, forcing a smile to his lips that doesn't quite reach his eyes. "Of course. We must keep trying."

I open my mouth to say something else, but there is a knock on the door. Nuwa sticks her head inside.

"Lady Liling is here, Your Majesties," she says. "I tried to send her away, but she insists on seeing you both."

I groan and don't try to hide it. She is the last person I want to see right now. If it were anyone else trying to push their way into my room at such as time, I'd summon the guards and have her dragged away. But since it is Lihua, I have to be careful not to make her too angry. I look pleadingly to Honghui, hoping that he will send her away. She can't retaliate against the emperor. But he misinterprets my look and tells Nuwa to admit Lihua.

"Your Majesties," Lihua says, entering the room and then bowing to us. "I'm so sorry about what has happened.

We had all hoped so much that it was true and a little prince was on the way."

"Yes," Honghui says. "It has been a disappointing morning."

"I'm sure," she says. "Which is why I have come, especially while the two of you are together. I thought it would cheer you to know that while the empress is not with child...I am."

"What?" Honghui and I both ask at the same time.

"Yes!" Lihua says, her face beaming. "It is true. I am with child. More than a month gone."

"Are you sure?" Honghui asks. It is clear that he is excited, but he is trying to restrain himself. He doesn't want to be disappointed again.

"Yes," she says. "I have all the signs: morning sickness, odd food cravings. I confirmed it with the midwife before she left."

Honghui lets out a long sigh of relief and looks to the ceiling. "Thanks be to Heaven!"

Lihua does not yet have a pregnancy belly, but still she puts her hands around her stomach protectively. "Are you not happy, Your Majesty?" she says to me.

In truth, I'm furious. It takes every ounce of my willpower not to jump out of bed and throttle her. How dare she bring such joyous news to me while I am still mourning the loss of my own child. I was never pregnant, I understand that, but I thought I was. I hoped I was. I thought that the symptoms would come. That I would soon feel the flutter of life within me that would confirm the belief that I was indeed pregnant. I might not have had a miscarriage, but I feel the loss just the same.

So, no, I am not happy. I am angry, and also fiercely jealous. I am the empress. I am Honghui's wife. I am the one who faced death just to be here. I am the one who upheld the secret that Lihua and I carry for years while she was in hiding. I am the one who should be pregnant. I have earned it.

"Get out," I mutter.

"What?" Lihua says as if she didn't hear me.

"Get out!" I yell.

"But...Your Majesty..." she says as though wounded.

"Daiyu," Honghui says. "This baby belongs to all of us."

"Get out!" I yell again. I grab a pillow and throw it across the room at Lihua. Honghui catches it.

"I'm sorry," Lihua says. "I thought the news would bring you joy, but it seems I am in error." She bows her way out of the room.

"Daiyu!" Honghui says. "That was poorly done. Don't you see? A baby truly is coming. You should be glad of it."

"Don't tell me how to feel," I say, and I can feel hot tears slipping down my cheeks. Tears of anger and sadness. Everything is going wrong.

"Fine," he says. "I will leave you until you are able to celebrate this pregnancy rationally."

"Then you'll leave me forever!" I yell at him as he leaves the room, slamming the door closed behind him. It was a stupid, hateful thing to say. The last thing I want is for a rift to form between myself and Honghui. But I can't explain to him why I feel the way that I do without telling him everything, and this is certainly not the time to do that.

19

———

"It was an honest mistake," Yanmei says, trying to reassure me. "It could have happened to any of us."

"I know," I say, trying, and probably failing, to disguise the bitterness in my voice. It has been a couple of weeks since I… I want to say since I lost the baby, but that is not what happened. It has been a couple of weeks since my monthly cycles resumed. Honghui has sent me gifts of jewelry and sweets and bolts of silk, and I have thanked him earnestly, but he has not summoned me to his bed, and I am not sure that I would go if he asked. I am not angry with him. It would not be fair of me to be so. But I am not ready to start trying to get pregnant again. In truth, I am not sure I want to have a child of my own. Oh, I understand the importance of a child, of the symbolism of one. If I were to fall pregnant, I would love it as much as possible. But I don't feel the innate desire to give birth the way other women do. I didn't feel it with Guozhi, and I still don't feel it with Honghui. I thought that I would. That being with a man of my choice would change my feelings on the matter, but it hasn't. In truth, I am content with being the mother of all the children born into the harem by the other women.

"I'm glad you're not pregnant," Dongmei says, not looking up from her paper cuttings.

"Really?" I ask, a little surprised. "Don't you want a little brother?"

"Of course," she says, still not looking up at me. "But I don't want you to die."

"Me neither," Jiangfei says. Jiangfei looks at me with big, wet eyes while Dongmei stays intent on her work. I place my hand on Jiangfei's back and kiss her head. The girls have still held me at a distance, but I believe their words are a good sign that they are learning to trust me again.

"That makes three of us," I say. "I am content to be your mother."

"Indeed," Yanmei says. "Let other women take the risk of childbirth. You have enough to keep you busy."

"My lady," a maid says, rushing to my side and kneeling.

"Yes?"

"Lady Liling is here," she says. "She wishes to see you."

"Of course," I say. As she goes to admit my guest, I have another maid clear off the table and bring over another chair. I stand to greet Liling, but when I see her, I nearly fall back into my seat.

"How is that possible?" I ask Lihua.

"What?" she asks innocently.

"That!" I say, pointing to her stomach.

"Oh!" she giggles and puts her hands around the slight but clearly visible round form that has already developed. According to her midwife, she is only around two months pregnant. Even my own mother did not show until she was four or five months along.

"My son seems to be developing quickly," Lihua says. "He will be healthy and strong, I'm sure."

"Maybe it is twins," Jiangfei says.

Lihua laughs again. "Two sons? That would surely be a blessing, wouldn't it?"

"Truly," I say through gritted teeth. But inside, my jealousy grows. Not jealousy that another woman should be pregnant with two sons by my husband. If the prospective mother in question were Yanmei, I would be nothing but joyful. Truly, should any of my husband's concubines fall pregnant, I would celebrate more loudly than anyone.

But why should it be Lihua? Why have the gods blessed her after all the turmoil she and her mother have put me through? If she does have a son, she will become a rank-two consort. When Honghui dies, she would be considered my equal as the new emperor's birth mother. In actuality, she would probably outrank me in the eyes of our son. I would become as Fenfeng, a mother in name only.

"I have brought you some tea, Your Majesty," Lihua says, motioning for her own maid to come forward with a tray of tea things. The maid places them on the table and sets to work preparing the tea for us to drink.

"Thank you," I say as I retake my seat, though I am not sure I can stomach anything right now. I'm not sure what it is, but I suddenly feel a bit nauseous. We were drinking tea and eating fruit before Lihua joined us, so I am sure it is not the tea that is making me feel unwell. It is surely Lihua herself that upsets me. Seeing her growing baby is not helping.

"Please, sit," I tell her, motioning toward the empty seat out of politeness, not because I actually want her to stay.

"How are you feeling?" Yanmei asks Lihua. I am glad that, as my chief lady-in-waiting and rank-three consort, she is able to take the lead in being polite and chatty when I cannot. "You look well."

"I feel fine," Lihua asks. "Well, I mean, there is always a bit of nausea when I wake up, but that passes after I drink some hot water. And it is already becoming difficult to walk on my pot-bottom shoes. I am afraid I shall have to switch to slippers soon."

"You should do so immediately," I say more harshly than I intended, but I am earnest in my words. "We would not have you fall and risk injury to yourself or his majesty's son."

Lihua's face falls for only a moment, as though surprised that I would dare censure her. But her smile quickly returns. "Yes, Your Majesty, you are quite right. I'll switch to slippers as soon as I return to my palace."

"There is no need to delay," I say. "What if you tripped on your walk from here to there. Why, you could slip here in my own garden. There is still a bit of mud around from the recent rains." I motion for Lihua's maid. "Go and fetch your lady's slippers right now."

"Yes, my lady," the maid says before scurrying away.

When I look back to Lihua, she is glaring at me and making no attempt to hide it. I can't help but smile. After all, I am in the right to be worried about the health and safety of the emperor's child.

"Have you felt the baby move?" Jiangfei asks as she reaches over to touch Lihua's belly. Lihua recoils suddenly and slaps Jiangfei's hand away. Jiangfei pulls her hand to her chest and tears fall from her eyes.

"Liling!" I say, pulling Jiangfei to me. "There was no need for that."

"I'm sorry," Lihua says. "It was just a reaction. I have to keep the baby safe."

"*Now* you worry about keeping the baby safe?" I ask. "I think that a little girl's touch is significantly safer than walking in pot-bottom shoes."

The maid returns at that moment with Lihua's slippers.

"You are right," Lihua says as the maid kneels down and changes Lihua's shoes. "I think I may have overexerted myself and am feeling a little overtired. If you don't mind, I am going to excuse myself."

"Of course," I say, more than a little glad to see her go. I can't help but chuckle to myself as she struggles to hold up her gown to keep it from dragging along the ground now that she is several inches shorter in her slippers than she was in her pot-bottom shoes. All of her clothes will have to be adjusted for the height difference now.

"I don't like her," Jiangfei says in a huff as she returns to her seat. "She might look like you, Mother, but she doesn't act like you."

I want to thank Jiangfei for her kind words toward me, but I know that I shouldn't encourage her to say such things.

"I am sure she is not herself," I say. "It is difficult being pregnant...or so I have heard."

"She's always been unpleasant," Dongmei says as she helps Yanmei pass around the cups of the tea Lihua left behind. "She's always around when we go and see Grandmother, but it is clear that she doesn't want us there."

I lick my lips as I wait for the tea to cool. I hadn't thought about using the girls to gather information for me about Fenfeng and Lihua. It still probably isn't a very good idea...

"She and the dowager empress are getting along?" I try to ask casually.

Dongmei shrugs. "I suppose, but they don't really talk

much. Whenever Fenfeng tries to talk to Liling, Liling just smiles and gives simple answers, if she replies at all."

"Hmm," is all I can say as I hold my teacup in both hands. So, it seems that Fenfeng is trying to talk to Lihua, trying to get information out of her, but Lihua is holding back. I have to wonder why. I mean, if Fenfeng was to learn the truth, that Lihua and I are not who we claim to be, that information could be just as damaging to Lihua as to me. So Lihua cannot be very forthcoming. Still, Lihua must see a benefit in serving Fenfeng instead of me. She seemed so eager to go to Fenfeng's household, but why? I simply cannot puzzle it all out.

"Yuck!" Dongmei says, practically throwing her teacup back to the table. "That tea is disgusting. What kind is it?"

Yanmei pulls a face and licks her lips as she puts her cup down more gracefully. "It is terribly bitter. Is it pu'er?"

I smell the tea. It is the same tea that Lihua had been serving me before. But I had never noticed how bitter it was. I mean, yes, it was always bitter, but I thought that was how it was supposed to taste and did my best to drink it down to be polite. But now, I can't hardly stomach it. I put my hand to my mouth to keep from vomiting.

"Take it away," I say to my maids. Nuwa comes over and sniffs the tea. "It is not familiar to me. Some kind of herb?"

Even after the tea is gone, my stomach continues to roil. Then, I feel a cramp, which is strange because my monthly cycle has passed. I then have a terrible thought.

What if it was the tea that caused my monthly bleed to cease? I grab Nuwa's arm, causing her to nearly spill the cup she is carrying.

"Find out what it is," I tell her.

"Very well," she says. "I'll ask Lady Liling presently."

"No," I say. "Take it to an apothecary. Ask him what it is."

Her eyes go large, and she looks to Yanmei.

"Your Majesty," Yanmei says. "You can't possibly think the tea is..." She looks at Dongmei and Jiangfei. Not wanting to upset them, she mouths the word *poison* at me.

"No," I say. "Of course not. I only want to know more about it. Learn its medicinal properties."

"Yes, my lady," Nuwa says. "I'll take care of it right away."

"What are you thinking?" Yanmei asks me.

I shake my head. "I'm not sure." I don't want to say anything until Nuwa learns more. But now that I think the tea might have been the reason for the false pregnancy, I can't let go of the idea. It would explain why my monthly bleed returned after Lihua left my household. She wasn't there to give me the tea every day. But why? Why would she want me to think I was pregnant? How did that benefit her?

I can't explain it, I just know that Lihua is much smarter than I am, far more devious and clever. If she is hatching some sort of plot against me, I'll never be able to figure it out until it is too late.

20

───────

The weeks pass, and Lihua's belly continues to grow. She cannot be elevated to a rank-two consort until she officially gives birth to a son, but she is still celebrated, nonetheless. This will be Emperor Honghui's first child, so even a daughter will be welcome. Gifts for Lihua and the emperor pour in from around the country. She is moved to a larger palace and her allowance is increased. Honghui visits her almost daily to check on her health and that of his son. I try to do my part, but my resentment toward Lihua only grows, and it is nearly impossible for me to hide my true feelings.

One night, I am lying in bed, trying to sleep, when I hear a noise from outside. I have always been a light sleeper with good hearing, so it does not surprise me to look down and see that Nuwa and Jinhai are still sleeping soundly. At first, I cannot tell what the sound is, so I close my eyes and listen. After a moment, it sounds like a woman humming. I suppose this should not surprise me. After all, the inner court is full of women—maids and ladies—so it should not seem odd that a woman is out at night. Perhaps it is simply someone else like me who cannot sleep. I tell myself to ignore whoever it is and go to sleep, but the humming continues. Slowly, the humming fades away, as if she is walking further away from my palace. For a moment, I remember how I first met my friend Wangli. She had been crying in the courtyard between our palaces. I feel a quick pain in my heart at the memory. How I miss Wangli and hope she is well and happy with her lover.

My curiosity gets the better of me, and I climb from the bed. It is autumn, and while the days are still pleasant, especially in the afternoons, the nights are quite cold and crisp. I put on some thick wool socks under my slippers and wrap a thick robe around myself before I pull the door to my bedroom open a crack. I make my way out of the palace and across the courtyard. I have to wait a moment for the guards to pass the gate on their patrol before I can exit the courtyard and try to find the singing lady. I had been able to hear her voice from my bedroom, so I head to that side of my palace.

At first, I hear nothing. I begin to think that she must be gone by now. Disappointed that I missed my chance at finding the girl, I start to turn back to my palace gate when my eyes drop to the ground and see small footprints in the dew that has sprouted on the paving stones. For some reason, the girl seems to not be wearing shoes. She must be freezing. I feel an urgency to my search as I follow the footsteps. Why would anyone be out on such a chill night without shoes? I don't want the girl to catch a chill or a cold or worse.

I follow the footsteps until they cross from a paved pathway to a wide expanse of grass that makes up one of the many palace gardens. I squint in the darkness to try and see who the footsteps belong to. Surely, since I could hear her from my bedroom window, she has not gotten too far ahead of me. Across the lawn, I see a flutter of white cloth reflecting the pale moonlight. I think it must be a young woman in a white sleeping gown.

"Hello!" I call out to her. What is she doing here? Is she not afraid of getting sick?

She glances toward me, but in the darkness and from such a distance, I cannot see who it is. I think she must see me, but instead of coming toward me, she turns and runs away.

"Wait!" I call as I bound across the grass after her. When I turn to follow her, I slip on the wet grass, getting my own sleeping gown muddy. But I right myself and keep running. I follow her down a corridor between several buildings, the path turning left, then right. I've completely lost sense of where I am until I come to a sudden stop.

Ahead of me is the Cold Palace. The abandoned palace is in even worse shape than the last time I saw it. Shudders have fallen from hinges. Ratty drapes flap in the breeze. The paving stones in front of it are cracked and uneven. The wooden slats of the two large doors are warped and gapped. Standing in front of the palace, with her back to me, is the woman in white.

"Who are you?" I call out. "What are you doing here?"

Slowly, she turns. My eyes fall to her arms, which are cradling her round belly. I let out a scream and lose my senses.

～

"*S*he's waking up!"

I open my eyes and see Nuwa and Yanmei fussing over me. I'm back in my own bed and there is a steaming cloth infused with herbs on my forehead.

"What's happened?" I ask, wondering if I've simply had a nightmare. But if that were true, why are there so many people around?

Honghui pushes Nuwa aside and sits next to me, taking my hand. He holds it to his cheek. "My darling, are you all right?"

"I...I don't know," I say, sitting up.

"What were you doing out there in the middle of the night?"

"I...I heard something," I say, trying to remember exactly what happened. "There was a woman, a woman dressed in white and she...she... Oh!" My hand goes to my mouth and I feel sick at the memory. "She was pregnant!"

"What?" Honghui asks. "Who was pregnant?"

"The woman in white," I say. "I could hear her singing outside my palace, so I followed her all the way to the Cold Palace. When she turned around so that I could see her, I could see that she was pregnant."

"But the only pregnant woman in the Forbidden City right now is Liling," Yanmei says.

"It wasn't Liling," I say. "At least, I don't think so." If it had been Lihua, I would have known immediately. Plus, if it had been her, why would she have run away from me? No, it wasn't her.

"Send someone to Liling's palace to make sure," Honghui says to no one in particular. A servant jumps up to fulfill the emperor's order. Honghui then turns back to me and runs his hand over my head and down my long hair. "Maybe it was just a nightmare. A figment of your imagination."

I shake my head. "No, I know what I saw. She was real. She was there. She was—" I gasp. Suddenly, I realize who it was. "It was Caihong!" As soon as the words leave my mouth, I wish I hadn't said them out loud.

Honghui's face falls and he recoils from me as though burned. "What? Caihong? Empress Caihong?"

"I...I don't know," I say, wishing I could take my words back. But as I think about the nightmare Caihong had before she died, how haunted by guilt as she was before her death, it makes sense to me that Caihong did not find peace after her death as I had hoped. She was outside the Cold Palace, the place where Lady An was banished. The place where Lady An hanged herself. A place where countless women have met their end after some sort of betrayal. But I say none of this to Honghui.

Honghui's face is grim and he presses his lips. "Daiyu," he finally says. "You have been under a lot of strain lately. I think, perhaps, you simply need to rest."

I shake my head. "Maybe it wasn't Caihong," I concede. "But I saw something, someone."

"It was just a dream," Honghui says.

I want to tell him that it wasn't. That I know what I saw. But do I? If I were speaking truthfully, I would say yes. Yes, I saw Empress Caihong outside the cold palace. I know it sounds crazy, but who else could it have been?

A maid enters the room. "Lady Liling says she has not left her palace all night, and her servants confirmed it."

"There," Honghui says. "See, if it wasn't Liling, who else could it have been? It was just a dream."

I let out a sigh and nod. "Yes, of course it was."

He kisses my forehead and takes his leave. "Just rest," he

says before closing the door to the room. Yanmei takes his place beside me on the bed.

"Did you really see Caihong's ghost?" she asks, her eyes wide.

"I don't know," I say. "I saw...someone. Something. Do you think it could be a bad omen?"

"You mean about Liling's child?" she asks. "Do you think something is going to happen to her?"

I shake my head, trying to force the bad thought away. "No. No, surely not. We can't think such things. Liling and her son will be fine."

"Yes, of course," Yanmei says. We are both quiet for a moment, afraid to speak our thoughts aloud.

"Take a bowl of rice and plate of food to the Cold Palace," I tell her. "Burn joss sticks and say a prayer."

Yanmei nods. "You wish to appease whatever hungry ghost could be haunting the place?"

I nod. "It might not have been Caihong, but I saw something. I don't know what the ghost wants, so we should make sure it is appeased before Liling's child is born."

"Yes, that is a good idea. I will take care of it..." She looks to the window and I notice it is not quite dawn yet.

"After daybreak," I tell her.

"Of course, Your Majesty," Yanmei says. She tucks my blanket around me and fluffs my pillows. "Now, you really should rest."

I try to give her a reassuring smile, but she must know that rest will be nearly impossible. I had always thought that Caihong's beliefs in dreams and hungry ghosts were old-fashioned superstitions. But now, I'm not so sure. I'm not even sure if what I saw was a ghost. She seemed more real than that. She left footprints on the ground. I had the feeling that she was trying to get away from me, not lead me somewhere. Could it be that there's another pregnant woman living within the walls of the Forbidden City, here in the inner court? On one hand, it seems impossible. But on the other, I suppose it is very possible. I have been told that the Forbidden City has a thousand buildings, so there must be many thousands of rooms. Someone could very easily hide here. But why would someone do that? Or am I simply grasping for an explanation when it is clear that I am being haunted by the ghost of Caihong? The birth of a new child could certainly be cause for her to return, to manifest herself. But why? Is she trying to tell me something? Why would she appear to me and not Lihua?

So many questions swirl through my head, making me dizzy. I finally do manage to close my eyes and find a little rest.

21

"Your Majesty, wake up."

"Hmm?" I moan.

It has been months since I have seen the ghost, or whoever she was. For weeks after, I had trouble sleeping. I would lie awake in my bed and listen for her humming voice to lure me from my bed. But slowly, as life returned to normal and everyone waited anxiously for Lihua's baby to be born, I nearly forgot all about her. But now, being woke in the middle of the night by Nuwa holding a lamp over my face, all of my fears come rushing back. I sit up quickly, nearly bumping my head on the lamp.

"What is it? What's wrong?" I ask.

"It is Lady Liling," she says. "The baby—"

I gasp and throw my blanket back, which takes a little work as it is now winter and there are four or five thick blankets piled upon me.

"Hurry! Summon the midwife," I say.

"My lady—"

"Has the emperor been notified?"

Your Majesty—"

"Where is my coat?"

"*My lady!*" Nuwa nearly yells to get my attention, stopping me in my tracks.

"What?" I ask her, and my heart seizes. "Oh no. Is something wrong? Has something happened?"

"No," Nuwa says. "Only that the baby is already here."

"What? What do you mean?"

"Apparently the birth was very quick and easy," Nuwa explains. "Her chief lady-in-waiting says that the wee thing merely slipped out and into the world before the midwife could even be summoned, though she is there now."

"And is it...alive?" I ask cautiously.

"Yes!" Nuwa says, a sudden, broad smile across her face. "A healthy boy!"

I reach out for a chair, but when I don't find one, I fall to the floor.

"My lady!" Nuwa rushes to my side. I haven't fainted, but all the strength seems to flee from me and I want to burst into tears. I *do* burst into tears. I don't know why. I knew the baby was coming. We all did. And all of us prayed every day that the baby would be a boy. But now that it has happened, that the precious baby boy, the heir and future emperor, has arrived, it is just too overwhelming.

"I'm sorry it wasn't you," Nuwa says as she wraps her arms around me and rocks me. I nod as I hold her and continue to cry. I let her believe that I am crying because I am jealous. I can't tell her the truth. That if the baby had been born to anyone else, I would be so glad. I would rejoice and sing the mother's praise from the golden rooftops of the Forbidden City.

"We must go and see the baby and check on the mother's well-being," I finally manage to say when my crying calms. I wipe the tears and snot away with my sleeve and Nuwa helps me stand. I start to pull my robe tight around me and tie it with a sash.

"You aren't planning to go and see her like that, are you?" Nuwa asks, horrified.

"Well, we should hurry," I say. "Surely everyone else is already present. I don't want people to think I am snubbing Liling and her child."

"You look a mess," Nuwa says, throwing open the door of my bed chamber and clapping her hands to get the other maids moving. "We will hurry. But if you go looking like you do, it will surely be seen as an insult. You should look your best to meet the little prince."

I suppose there is some truth to her words, both for the reasons she says, and the reasons she doesn't. It would appear as if I don't care about the momentousness of the occasion if I did not take some care with my appearance. But also, I need to remind those around me that I am still the empress. With the birth of a baby boy, Lihua will be elevated to rank-two consort. She will be second in power and respect only to me. Some people will even see her as outranking me since she is the birthmother to the future emperor. I will need to work hard to ensure my place within the inner court.

Since it is the middle of the night and we are in a hurry, Nuwa styles my hair quickly and puts on only the most essential of makeup. But she tops my head with my phoenix crown, usually only worn for official occasions, which I suppose this is, and wraps me in a sumptuous yellow robe embroidered with the symbol for longevity. Even as a rank-two consort, Lihua will not be allowed to wear the shade of yellow that is reserved for the emperor and empress.

Finally, I am deemed ready, and I climb into a sedan chair to be carried to Lihua's palace. The night air is cold and damp. It is not quite raining, but a wet mist hangs in the air and moistens my face. As I suspected, I think the entire palace has arrived ahead of me. All of the palace's servants surround the palace and sing songs, perform kowtows, and praise Heaven for such a marvelous blessing. The other concubines and their maids are in the courtyard since they cannot all fit inside the palace. All of them, though, seem near to tears instead of brimming with joy. They all bow when they see me.

"I know how each of you feel," I tell them as I bid them to rise. "But this child does not belong only to Liling, but to all of us. We are all mothers this day." I say words that I know I am supposed to say, but I also know how hollow they must ring inside the hearts of women who so long to have a child of their own.

"Your time will come," I tell them. "I am sure of it. We have a healthy son on this day. Surely more children are to follow." They all nod and murmur in agreement at this, and I hope I am right. Why wouldn't I be? If Honghui can have one son, surely he can father many more children.

I hold my hand out to Yanmei. "Come with me," I whisper to her. "I need you by my side."

Her eyes are glassy as she nods to me and squeezes my hand. "Be strong," she says. I nod and let out a few calming breaths. Finally, I can delay no longer.

As I enter Lihua's palace, smoke from incense burns my eyes and clouds my vision, the sickly sweetness filling my nose and making my stomach churn. I can hear a priest chanting from somewhere in the building. The palace is crowded with maids and eunuchs waiting to attend Lihua, the emperor, and the dowager empress. They all part when they see me, giving me a clear path to Lihua's bed chamber.

Even though it is night, Lihua's room is lit up bright as day with lanterns, candles, and a brazier in the middle of the room that also gives off plenty of heat. Along with the countless people in the room, the room is stifling hot, causing me to break out into a sweat.

"Your Majesty!" Lihua calls to me from her place on her bed, looking radiant and refreshed. I helped my mother deliver each of my sisters, so I know how a woman usually looks after giving birth. It is an exhausting and painful ordeal, and it can take the mother days to recover, more if the birth was difficult. I know that Nuwa said that Lihua had an easy birth, but still, she does not look like a woman who just forced another human being out of her. Her hair is brushed smooth and lays delicately over her shoulders. Her cheeks are pink with happiness and she seems unable to stop smiling. Her legs are covered with a blanket, but it appears as if her stomach has already gone mostly flat.

But I hardly have time to wonder of Lihua's quick recovery. Honghui turns to me, tears of joy streaming down his face, as he holds a little bundle in his arms.

"Daiyu!" he says. "I have a son. Come and see."

I let go of Yanmei's hand and cross over to stand in front of my husband. He lowers the bundle and moves the folds of blankets aside to reveal a tiny, pink face. The baby is sleeping soundly, and I can see his nostrils flaring slightly with each quiet breath. He has a little tuft of thick black hair on the top of his head, and I can see the rough patch on his forehead that many infants have that indicate their journey into the world.

Honghui lowers his face to that of his son. He takes in

his scent and kisses the baby's head. "Would you like to hold him?" he asks me.

I realize I have almost no feeling in my arms. My whole body feels numb. It is as if I am present only in my mind but left my body behind in my own palace. Still, I nod, since I know it will seem strange if I don't want to hold the baby. After all, this is supposed to be my baby too. I am Honghui's only true wife, so his children are my children.

I held each one of my sisters the instant they were born, even before my mother held them, so I am no stranger to holding a newly born babe. And yet, as Honghui hands his son to me, my arms shake so badly I fear I will drop him.

"Help me. Help me," I utter to Honghui, and his warm hands remain under my arms to help support me.

"Isn't he wonderful?" Honghui says. I can say nothing, but of course he is. He is beautiful. He is healthy. He is a boy. He is everything Honghui needs in a child.

"He is perfect," I hear Fenfeng say. I had tried to ignore her presence, but I raise my head to see her hovering just next to Honghui's shoulder.

"Thank you, Mother," Honghui says, and I hear nothing but sincerity in his voice. Fenfeng preens under his words.

"You are already a wonderful father," Fenfeng says. "And Liling has done her duty to perfection. Could you ever ask for more in a woman?"

"No, I couldn't," Honghui says. He looks to Lihua. "Thank you, my love. I shall forever be grateful to you."

Lihua lowers her head humbly under Honghui's praise.

"Why, she looks ready to give you another son almost immediately," Fenfeng says with a laugh.

"I look forward to trying," he says in reply.

I can take it no longer and hand the baby back to Honghui before my strength goes out of me completely. He called Lihua his love. He wants to have her in his bed. She is perfection. Where does that leave me? Part of me knows that Honghui isn't thinking clearly or speaking his true feelings. He is overcome with emotion in the moment. He is delirious in the joy of holding his son for the first time. And yet his words hurt, cutting me deep in the most insecure parts of myself.

"Your Majesty," Lihua says, looking at me with a pained expression on her face. "Are you not pleased with me?"

I open my mouth to respond, but Fenfeng speaks first.

"Jealousy is most unbecoming in a woman," she says, shaking her head. "And at such a happy time! How can you ruin this moment for the emperor?"

"I'm not," I say, growing frustrated.

"Perhaps you should leave," Honghui says to me.

"What?" I ask in shock. "You cannot think so poorly of me."

"I just want to enjoy this moment," he says in exasperation. I look around the room, and while Nuwa and Yanmei appear sympathetic to me, they are the only ones. Fenfeng and Lihua look disappointed while all their servants look almost angry with me, disgusted. I have to get away from this place. I give a quick bow and then leave the room. But outside the bed chamber, still, I find more angry faces. I think I even hear voices mumbling about jealousy and anger and what a poor example of an empress I am. I rush past them, not waiting for Nuwa or Yanmei.

Outside the palace, a light drizzle has started to fall. The other concubines stand in the rain and cold, looking as if they are melting as their makeup runs and their hair falls around their faces. They look to me for hope, for reassurance, but I can give them none. I step down to the walkway and slip on the water in my pot-bottom shoes. I hear my gown rip and feel my headdress totter.

"Empress!" Nuwa rushes to my side. For some reason, her words strike my heart.

"I am not worthy of being an empress!" I say. I kick off my shoes and rip the headdress from my hair, tossing it into a puddle. I lift the hem of my gown and run from Lihua's palace. I have to get away from here. I need to be alone. Why did Lihua have to come here? Why did she have to disturb the little bit of happiness that I had found?

I run across a grassy lawn and my feet sink in the mud. I slip and land on my knees and I know my glorious yellow robe is ruined. I tug at the sash around my waist so I can remove the robe altogether, leaving it in the muddy garden so I can walk more easily. The night is cold, and I can see my hot breath collect in front of me. I hold my head up to the moon and let the rain trickle over my face, down my neck, and over my body.

I hear voices and look toward them, expecting to see Nuwa or perhaps Jinhai looking for me. But that is not who I see. Instead, I see four eunuchs all dressed in dark clothes. Their wide-brimmed straw hats shield the moonlight, shrouding their faces in shadow. I start to turn away, thinking they must be completing nighttime chores, when I realize that all four of them are carrying something between them. Something heavy. Something long wrapped in a white sheet. I cannot help but walk toward them to see what they are doing. They seem to be arguing, motioning this way and that, as if they are unsure which way to go. They finally come to a consensus and turn away from me, trotting off quickly. I realize that they will soon be beyond my reach, so I call out to them.

"Hey! Stop!"

One of the men toward the back of the group lifts his head, as if he isn't sure what he heard, but he then slows his pace and looks over his shoulder at me. He screams and drops his corner of the sheet.

"Ghost!" he yells, pointing toward me. The other three men stop and look at me, they all scream and scatter, dropping their load. One of the men tries to gather the others back together, calling them fools and idiots. But as I get closer, he too cries out for Heaven to save him as he runs away. For a moment, I wonder why they think I am a ghost, but as I look down, I realize that without my outer robe, I am only wearing a long, white shift. And drenched in rain as I am, I hardly look like the empress I am supposed to be. But I can't enjoy the humor in the moment as I get closer to whatever it is that the men have dropped.

It is clear to me before I even reach the spot that the men were carrying a body. The white sheet reveals the unmistakable shape. But who is it? And why would they be carrying such a thing away in the middle of the night? If it were a maid or eunuch, Fiyanggu should be making sure the body is disposed of properly, but I am sure he was not among the men I saw.

I kneel beside the body and pull the edge of the cloth back. I shriek and fall back when I see the face of a woman —a woman who looks very much like me. I then realize that she is the woman I saw the night I saw the ghost. I thought that I had not seen her face clearly that night, but I now realize it is because I was looking at myself. Though, she does not look exactly like me, only similar. Perhaps as similar as I look to Lihua.

So, she was not a ghost, but a real woman. I then remember that she had been pregnant, so I pull the sheet back further. Her stomach is smaller, but still round, as if she has recently given birth. The lower part of her dress is bloody, as if she is still wearing her birthing clothes.

Who is she? Why is she here? Why is she dead? Where is her baby?

All of these thoughts are swirling through my mind when I feel a sudden sharp pain in the back of my head, and everything goes black.

22

———

It takes a great effort to open my eyes, as if they are weighted down with heavy stones. When I finally do manage to pry them open, I see that the room is mostly dark, save the flickering flames from the brazier in the middle of the room. I turn my head to see if anyone is in the room with me and wince. It feels as though someone has stabbed me through the brain and left the blade behind. I lie still and let out a moan of pain.

"Your Majesty!" Nuwa appears by my side from somewhere. The pain in my head makes it hard for me to focus. "Go tell the emperor that she is awake!" Nuwa tells someone else in the room.

"What...what happened?" I ask her.

"I was going to ask you the same thing," she says, dabbing my face with a warm cloth.

"What do you mean?" Her words aren't making sense to me. If someone found me, they must have some idea of what happened.

"Jinhai went to find you after you ran off," Nuwa says. "He said he found you on the ground in the rain and that there was a bloody lump on the back of your head. He thought you were dead."

"Someone hit me?" I ask.

"Don't you remember?"

I start to shake my head, but that is a mistake. I put my hand to my head, partly over my eyes. Even though the light from the brazier is soft, it is still too much.

"I felt a pain," I say. "I didn't see who or what it was."

"What about before that?" Nuwa asks.

"Oh, right," I say as I try to think for a moment. "I went for a walk. Or maybe a run. I don't know. I just needed to get away from...from..." I stop myself from saying her name because I can't remember it for the moment. I want to say Lihua, but I feel as though that isn't right. I know it isn't. But I can't come up with the correct name.

"In the rain?" Nuwa asks. "You could catch a chill, or worse."

"I know," I say. "I wasn't thinking clearly."

Nuwa nods but doesn't press the issue. "Then what?"

"I saw...I saw..." I close my eyes tightly and try to remember. "Her."

"Who?" Nuwa asks.

I suck in a breath. "Her! The ghost!"

Nuwa gasps, her hand to her mouth. "You saw her again? Did you follow her?"

"No," I say. "She was dead."

Nuwa is quiet for a long moment. I open my eyes and see that she looks confused. It is as if she almost wants to laugh, as though I made a joke of some sort.

"What?" I ask.

"Well, she is a ghost," Nuwa says. "Of course she is dead."

"No," I say. "She's not a ghost. I mean, at least she wasn't. Maybe she is now."

"Your Majesty," Nuwa says, growing exasperated. "You aren't making any sense."

There is a commotion from somewhere, and the door to the room flies open. Honghui is standing there, his face flushed. He rushes to my side and takes my hand.

"My love," he says, kissing my hand. "What happened? Who did this to you?"

"It was the ghost," I say.

"What?" Honghui looks to Nuwa, who only shrugs and shakes her head. "What do you mean?" he asks me more slowly.

"I saw her," I say. "The ghost woman. Only she wasn't a ghost. She was a woman, a real woman. But she was dead."

"But...you said she wasn't a ghost," Honghui says, putting the back of his hand to my forehead as if checking for a fever. Maybe he thinks I am delusional. Maybe I am. Even I am confused right now. And my head is throbbing in pain.

"When I saw her before," I say, trying to explain. "I thought she was a ghost. But now, I think she was alive. But when I saw her last night, she was dead."

"What makes you think she was dead?" Honghui asks, and I hope he is finally understanding me.

"She looked dead," I say. "She was wrapped in a white sheet."

"Where did you see her?" he asks.

"I don't know," I say. "In the rain. Probably wherever you found me."

Honghui sighs and rubs his own forehead. "You were alone when we found you. No one else was there, certainly not a dead woman."

"They must have carried her off," I say.

"Who?"

"The eunuchs," I say. "There were four eunuchs carrying the body wrapped in the white sheet."

At this, Honghui's face looks a little lighter, and I think I must be making more sense. My head is still in a lot of pain, but it feels a little more clear.

"Who were they?" Honghui asks. "Did you recognize them?"

I close my eyes again and try to remember the scene. I shake my head. "It was too dark. Their hats shadowed their faces."

"But you are sure you saw four eunuchs carrying a body wrapped in a white sheet?" he asks.

"Yes," I say.

"How did you get close enough to see the body?"

"When the men saw me, they dropped her and ran away," I say. "I think they were afraid of me."

"Then what happened?"

I wanted to see what they were carrying, so I went over and pulled the sheet back. That was when I saw her."

"The ghost woman," Honghui says. "The woman you saw before outside the Cold Palace."

"Yes," I say. "It was her. I'm sure of it."

"But I thought you said the ghost woman was Caihong."

"Well, I assumed it was Caihong," I say. "I didn't get a clear look at the woman's face. But who else would be haunting me?"

"If you didn't see her face, then how do you know the woman you saw last night was the same ghost woman?" Honghui asks. His question is reasonable, but it makes me angry.

"I just know," I say.

Honghui presses his lips and looks away for a moment. I'm afraid he doesn't believe me, but he doesn't want to tell me that he doesn't.

"Who hit you over the head?" he asks. I'd been so focused on the ghost woman, I nearly forgot about that part. I reach up and lightly touch the back of my head. I wince because it is still extremely tender.

"I don't know," I say. "I was looking down at the body of the dead woman. But it must have been one of the eunuchs who had been carrying her. They ran off, but they must have come back and I didn't hear them."

Honghui nods thoughtfully. "We will find out who did this to you." He leans forward and kisses me on the forehead so lightly, I barely feel it. "Please, rest."

"I will," I tell him. He stands up and storms out of the room with a purpose. After all, whether or not I am right about seeing a ghost or a dead body, someone did attack me. *Me!* The empress of China. And attacked me within the supposedly safe walls of the Forbidden City. That is a crime that cannot go unanswered for.

I lean back on my pillow, but that hurts the back of my head, so I turn over and lie on my side, watching the door. Nuwa returns with a tray of tea things.

"I'll make a calming brew to help you sleep," she says.

"Thank you." I would like to rest, at least long enough for the pain to go away. My mind is still foggy, groggy, confused, yet it still tries to make some sense of what I saw.

If I did indeed see the body of a dead woman, who was she? Why was she there? Who killed her? Or did she die in childbirth? What happened to her baby? It seems a strange coincidence that she should die on the same night that Lihua gave birth.

I have to turn away from Nuwa and face the blank, dark

wall as thoughts start to come together. Watching Nuwa prepare the tea is too distracting in my injured state. If the woman died giving birth on the same night that Lihua gave birth, did that mean that there were now two babies within the Forbidden City?

"Nuwa?" I say, not looking at her. "Have any maids recently given birth?"

"A kitchen maid gave birth about three weeks ago at her mother's home," she says. "And I heard that one of Lady Xiuying's maids was given leave to marry and is already with child. I suppose she will not be returning."

"But no one has done so recently?" I push. "Not within the Forbidden City or inner court."

"Gracious, no!" she says. "Any working woman within the Forbidden City is sent home to give birth."

Then where is the baby? I ask myself, my teeth clenched tightly closed. The answer seems so close.

It's Lihua's baby is the answer that comes to me. I try to push it away. It's too ludicrous to believe. But at the same time, it's the only answer that makes sense. After all, Lihua gave birth without anyone present save her own maid. What I mean is, she didn't give birth at all. She claimed she gave birth and presented the ghost lady's baby as her own.

Lihua was never pregnant.

I sit up sharply and scream out in pain.

"Your Majesty!" Nuwa yells, grabbing my shoulders and trying to force me to lay down.

"No! No!" I cry out. "I must get up. I must see!"

"Must see what?" she asks.

"The baby!" I say. "I must see the baby."

"Oh, my lady," Nuwa says pitifully. "Yes, of course. I understand. But the child and his mother must rest now. As should you. Please, sleep, and you can visit him in the morning."

No, I must see him now, but I know that Nuwa will not permit me to leave my bed. But I must go see him, must look upon his face once again. I was so overcome with emotion, I didn't look closely enough at his face. Did he look like Honghui? Does he look like the emperor's son? I must know!

"Please," I beg Nuwa. "I need more than tea. My head. My head!"

"Yes, of course, my lady!" Nuwa says. "I'll go fetch a doctor right away." She jumps up and heads to the door, barking orders to the maids and eunuchs who must be standing around in need of something to do. I hear the front door to the palace open and think that Nuwa must have gone to fetch the doctor herself. She would not rely on a lower-ranking maid for such an important task.

My head is still in terrible pain, but I need to try and sneak out while I can. I climb from my bed and throw on a red robe, then slip my feet into leather slippers. It is wet out and I have already spent too much time in the elements without protection. If I am not careful, I really will catch a chill.

I open the door to my room and see that the outer room is empty. It is the middle of the night, so I assume that most of my household is sleeping. Those on duty must be busy with whatever tasks Nuwa set them to. Before I can talk myself out of it, I cross the room and slip out the front door. I then cross the courtyard and make my way through the gate and across the nearest garden in order to avoid any patrolling guards. I don't want anyone to try and stop me from seeing the baby. I have to see him. I must know the truth.

When I arrive at Lihua's palace, I am exhausted and my head is dizzy, but I cannot give up. Her guards approach me, but I tell them to go away. I am the empress, after all. They cannot tell me where I can and cannot go. They answer to me. The same with all of Lihua's servants. They are all surprised to see me, but they cannot stop me. I dismiss her maids and eunuchs and enter the room where the little prince has been set up. A wet nurse is holding the baby, walking around the room, bouncing him to help him sleep.

"Your Majesty!" She takes a step back so quickly when she sees me, I fear she will stumble.

"Give me the baby!" I order her. She hesitates. I'm sure I look affright, but she has no right to deny me what I ask. "Give me my son!" I practically yell.

The wet nurse's hands shake as she hands the baby over to me, but mine are steady. The baby cries, his mouth gaping like a little fish looking for food. Unfortunately, I have no food to give him, and I wonder if Lihua does either. I put my knuckle to his mouth to settle him and make a soft shushing sound. He is a pretty little thing. His mouth is a perfect little bow and his cheeks are full.

But he doesn't look like Honghui.

Still, I suppose that isn't proof that he is not Honghui's son. Dongmei didn't really favor Guozhi. In fact, now that I think about it, she looks like Honghui—

The realization hits me so hard, I fall to my knees. I hold tightly to the baby so that I don't drop him, but he is suddenly far less important to me.

Dongmei. Honghui. Lady An.

And Guozhi knew. That was why he despised Lady An so much. Dongmei is Honghui's daughter. How could I have been so blind? Why did not I not know? Why did no one ever tell me?

I hear a scream from behind me. I turn and see Lihua. But her face is...strange. She is screaming, but it looks as if she is smiling, laughing even.

"Help!" she cries out. "The empress is trying to hurt my baby!"

23

"What?" I cry out. At first, her words don't make any sense. Who is trying to hurt the baby? I look around, but Lihua and I are the only ones in the room.

"Stop! Help!" she yells, then she approaches me with outstretched arms. "Please, give the baby to me. Don't hurt him."

"What? Me?" I say, pushing myself to my feet awkwardly with the infant still in my arms. "I'm not hurting him. I'm just trying to look at him."

Lihua screams. "No! Please, please, please. I'll do anything."

"What are you blabbering about?" I ask, stomping my foot. "I'm not hurting the baby, I'm just trying to look at his face."

Lihua's own face drops for a moment, but just then, several guards rush into the room.

"Oh, thank Heaven," Lihua says, pointing toward me with a shaky hand. "Please, save my baby. She's going to hurt him."

The guards hesitate, looking between Lihua and me.

"Stop her!" Lihua orders, her voice firm and, frankly, terrifying.

One of the guards steps toward me, reaching for the baby.

"Don't you dare touch me," I say, holding the baby even more tightly to my chest. I can feel him start to squirm. I'm sure he doesn't appreciate all the commotion around him as he tries to sleep.

The guard recoils, looking to his fellow guard, who only shrugs.

"She's going to hurt my baby!" Lihua says. "She's jealous and wants to kill him."

"Stop this!" I tell Lihua, but she only starts crying hysterically.

"My baby! My precious baby! Please don't hurt him."

"What is going on in here?" Emperor Honghui enters the room suddenly, and everyone drops to their knees. "Daiyu, what are you doing in here?"

"She's trying to hurt my baby!" Lihua cries before I can speak. "I entered the room and she was trying to smother him with a pillow."

"That's a lie!" I say. "I was only holding him."

"She's jealous, Your Majesty," Lihua says, grabbing one of Honghui's hands and tugging on it. "You saw how she acted earlier when she was here, the way she ran away. She couldn't even pay us the proper respect, she is so consumed with jealousy."

The baby starts to cry. I look down at him and try to comfort him with calming sounds and bouncing. I try to get another look at his face, try to see his father in him, but with his face screwed up and turning red, he looks like a little underworld creature instead of a person.

"Daiyu," Honghui says, stepping toward me and holding his hand out, "give me the baby."

"Your Majesty," I say, "I would never—"

"Give him to me!" Honghui commands. I hold the crying bundle out to him, and he takes it from me quickly. My heart hurts, the pain throbbing.

"Do you really think me capable of hurting a child?" I ask. "How could you think such a thing of me?"

Honghui hands the baby to Lihua, who leaves the room, coddling her child. Well, I'm still not convinced that it is her child at this point.

"Daiyu," Honghui says with a frustrated sigh. "You have not been yourself lately."

"What are you talking about?"

"It is clear that you are jealous of Liling and her son," Honghui says.

"I am not!" I say, tugging on my hair.

"Then why are you acting this way?" he asks.

"I'm not acting any way," I say.

"Really?" Honghui asks. "Running around at night. Seeing ghosts and dead bodies. The way you've been treating Liling. You've been acting crazy!"

"I am *not* crazy," I say, his words hurting me more and more. "I thought you loved me." My eyes are tearing up.

"I do love you," he says.

If that is true, I want to ask him why he never told me he was Dongmei's father. I want to know the truth. But then I remember the night we first met. The night he was sneaking out of the Forbidden City. The night I was trying to sneak back in because I had foolishly left in an attempt to find my family. If I ask him to tell me the truth, if he had been with Lady An earlier that night, if they were lovers, then it will remind him that I've kept secrets from him too. That I've been lying too. If I force him to tell me the truth about Dongmei, then he might insist that I tell him the truth about who I am, and I'm not sure I can risk that right now. He already thinks I'm acting crazy.

Maybe I am acting crazy. Maybe I *am* crazy.

Did I really see a ghost woman in the middle of the night? Did I really see a group of eunuchs carrying a dead body around? Do I really think that Lihua's baby is someone else's? Ever since I thought I was pregnant, my mind has been so unsettled. Nightmares, fears, jealousy. All of it has plagued me, disrupted what I thought was to be a happy, peaceful time in my life.

"What is wrong with me?" I ask Honghui helplessly.

"I don't know," he says. "I can understand you feeling jealous."

I have to tsk my tongue at that and turn away. I hate when he says that because I truly don't feel that way. At least, not in the way he thinks. I'm not jealous of Lihua—I'm distrustful of her.

"Then why did you come here in the middle of the night?" Honghui asks. "You are exhausted and injured. Why didn't you stay in your room? Why are you here?"

"Because I don't think that is your son," I say. He steps back, his mouth open. Part of me regrets telling him what I really think. But another part of me is relieved. If the baby isn't his son, then he needs to know the truth. He can't make the child his heir.

"What are you talking about?" he asks.

"If the woman I saw was real and not a ghost, then who was she? Why was she here?"

"It was just a dream," he says.

"No," I insist. "I saw her. I'm sure of it."

"The woman who you thought was Caihong."

"Stop saying that," I say. "I can admit when I am wrong, and I was wrong about that. But I'm not wrong about seeing *someone* that night. Someone who was pregnant. Someone who I then saw dead."

"Enough!" Honghui says. "Guards!"

"Listen to me!" I try.

"No," Honghui says as two guards enter the room. "You are injured and exhausted. Your mind isn't right. I have asked you to rest, now I am ordering you to do so."

Honghui then turns to the guards. "Take the empress back to her palace. Set guards outside her room and her palace gate at all times. Even during patrols, her doors and gate are not to be left unattended. Do you understand?"

"Yes, Your Majesty," the men say. They then step toward me, no hesitation this time. The emperor's word is law in all things. Even as the empress, my words are useless against his.

"Don't touch me!" I tell them as they reach for my arms. "I can walk on my own." I'll not let them drag me away like a prisoner or crazy woman. The guards look at the emperor for confirmation, and he nods.

"*Escort* the empress home," Honghui clarifies.

"Yes, Your Majesty," they say in unison.

I hold my chin up as I walk past Honghui and out of the room. In the main room, Lihua is there holding her baby protectively. All of her servants are there as well. I am sure that the servants heard the entirety of my conversation with Honghui. Soon, everyone in the Forbidden City will know that the emperor called me crazy. And since his word is considered truth, people might start to believe him.

The guards walk behind me close enough to step on my heels all the way back to my palace. When I get there, Nuwa and Yanmei rush out to meet me.

"Where have you been?" Yanmei asks, taking my hand.

"What's going on?" Nuwa eyes the guards warily.

I shake my head as we walk inside. "I've made a terrible mistake."

"What's wrong?" Yanmei asks again. She leads me to my room and helps me change into clean, warm clothes. Settled back in my own bed, the exhaustion overtaking me, I can't stop myself from crying.

"Oh, Yanmei," I say. "I think I'm losing my mind."

"No, certainly not," she says as she takes a handkerchief and dabs at my eyes. "Why would you say that?"

"Do you believe that I saw the ghost woman?" I ask.

Yanmei fusses with my blanket as she thinks on how to answer, which tells me that she does not, in fact, believe me.

"I'm sure you saw something," Yanmei answers tactfully.

"But not a ghost?" I push. I don't know why I'm punishing her this way. None of it is Yanmei's fault. But she is my dearest, oldest, and most loyal friend. If even she does not believe me, what chance do I have that anyone else will?

"How can I say when I was not there?" Yanmei replies, her tone even. "It could have been a maid or a dream or a ghost. I don't know. Even if I had been with you, I might not have seen it if the ghost only wanted to appear to you.

"That is why I say that I believe you saw something. I don't think you are crazy. But only you know what you saw."

"You don't think I'm crazy?" I repeat, needing to hear her say the words more than I realized.

"No!" she says, and this time, she doesn't hesitate.

I let out a sigh of relief. "Yanmei, you know that Liling is not to be trusted, right?"

Yanmei nods. "I know that she holds some sort of power over you, and that is what makes me not trust her."

"Is it possible that the baby, the little prince, is not her son?" I ask. Yanmei's eyes go big. Of course, it is an idea she never would have considered before. "I'm beginning to think that the ghost woman I saw was not a ghost at all, but a real woman. A pregnant woman. I think she gave birth and that Liling claimed her baby as her own."

"That is a very dangerous accusation," Yanmei says quietly.

"I know. I know," I say, rubbing my forehead.

"But...if you have proof..." Yanmei looks at me hopefully.

"Only what I saw," I say. "I saw four eunuchs carrying the dead body of the ghost woman. So, she wasn't a ghost, she was real, and she was pregnant. But now she's dead and her baby is gone."

Yanmei turns away for a moment to think. She finally shakes her head. "But you have no proof. You cannot say such a thing without proof."

"I know," I say.

Yanmei kneels by my bed and squeezes my hand tight. "Daiyu, you know that even if Liling has a son, a true son of her own, it is not the end for you. I don't know what power she has over you, but the only true power in the Forbidden City is that of the emperor. As long as you have his love, his favor, you will be his empress.

"Her son is only his heir because he is the only son Honghui has. Put Liling out of your mind, I beg of you. Focus on Honghui. Give him a son. He will surely favor a son by you above any other. It is your son who will be emperor."

"Or yours," I say.

"Anyone's son!" Yanmei says. "It is clear that he does not favor Liling. He pays her the respect she is owed, but nothing more. Please, I beg you, for your own sake, focus on Honghui and forget Liling."

I nod at Yanmei's wise words. She is right, of course. At least, to an extent. As long as Honghui is happy with me, there is little Liling could do to hurt me. Especially now, since she will be busy with her new baby. I can't prove that her son is not Honghui's child, so I cannot allow the possibility to trouble my mind.

"You are right," I tell Yanmei. "I will do my best."

"How is your head?" she asks. I reach up and lightly touch the back of it. I grimace when I feel the soft spot.

"Still tender," I say.

"Rest," Yanmei says. "Lie on your side and sleep for as long as you need."

I look to the window and see that the sun is rising. Yanmei notices it as well.

"Sleep all day and night if you must," she says.

"I will," I say.

Yanmei fluffs my pillows and smooths my blanket before kissing me on my forehead and closing the door to my room behind her. I snuggle down into my bed and close my eyes, determined to sleep. But all I can see in the darkness of my mind is the face of the ghost woman who is missing her baby.

24

———

"So, will the little prince have a baby brother or sister soon?" Xiuying asks, looking around at me and the other consorts as we sit in a circle and embroider together in the warmth of my sitting room. Everyone is present except Lihua. Since the weather is cold, the doctors have advised her not to leave her palace as much as possible.

The women giggle and blush. Honghui seems eager to have another child as soon as possible, taking a woman to his bed every night. Even I have been to his bed chamber recently. My heart and mind are still troubled. I fear letting my guard down and worry about Lihua constantly, but I do my best to keep my thoughts and feelings to myself, pressed way down deep inside my gut so that no one else knows how I really feel. After all, Yanmei is right. Keeping Honghui happy is paramount. If he is happy, that is when I am safest, no matter what Lihua might do.

"I am sure Heaven will bless us soon," I say. Though why none of the girls are pregnant yet, I have no idea. Of course, if Lihua's child is not Honghui's, it could be because he is incapable of having children. But then I remember that Dongmei is his daughter—I'm sure of it—so he is certainly capable. It will just take time.

"Actually…" Yanmei says, not looking up from her embroidery, "I'm pregnant."

Everyone gasps and shrieks. Some clap their hands and several girls rush over to Yanmei's side to touch her still-flat belly. But then, everyone seems to remember that I am present and they all go silent, looking at me for my response.

"Are you sure?" I ask her. I think back to the many months that I thought I was pregnant and am hesitant to be anything more than skeptical just yet.

"Yes," she says. "I've had three doctors and two midwives confirm it."

"What?" I ask. "How did you manage to do so in secret?"

"It wasn't exactly secret," Yanmei says. "His majesty knew. We arranged for the doctors to come and examine me on nights that he summoned me to his bed. We didn't want anyone in the inner court to know until we were certain." She looks at me, her eyes wary.

"You mean, you didn't want me to know," I say.

She shakes her head. "I didn't want to worry you. I didn't want to upset you."

"Oh, Yanmei," I say, tears coming to my eyes. "You know that I couldn't be happier." We both stand up and hug each other tightly. There is a sigh of relief among the other ladies, and then there is much cheering and celebrating.

I feel immense relief as well. Of course, part of me is hurt that some people thought that I would react badly to Yanmei's announcement. But then, they had no reason to think I would react otherwise. I did react badly to Lihua's pregnancy and birth, there is no denying that. And no one but Yanmei knows the truth of why. Almost everyone thought that I was reacting out of pure jealousy. They didn't realize how afraid I was. But this is my chance to set everything right. To show everyone that I am not jealous but am truly happy for both Yanmei and Honghui.

I immediately send a note of congratulations to Honghui and to Fenfeng. In fact, I go so far as to invite Fenfeng to my palace to celebrate. She declines the invitation but sends a bolt of silk to Yanmei in imperial yellow to start making clothes for the baby.

I take the lead in honoring Yanmei, organizing her move to a larger palace—that also happens to be closer to mine—and work with Fiyanggu to increase Yanmei's allowance and hire more servants. Honghui praises me for my positive attitude and the good example I am setting for all women. While everyone is happy that a new child is on the way, it is clear that some of the other concubines are disappointed that they have once again been passed over by the gods for such a blessing. I do my best to comfort them and pressure Fiyanggu to make sure all of the women are rotated equally as Honghui's bedmate. I make sure that the women are not wasting their money on bribes by overseeing Honghui's schedule personally.

I know that Lihua is frustrated. I avoid talking to her as much as possible, but when I do, her face is usually sour. Even though she should have everything her heart desires, she complains that she has not be invited back to Honghui's bed. That, however, is beyond my control. Tradition dictates that she not be touched by her husband for six months after the birth of her child. I try to use this to my advantage, though. I hope that as many of the concubines as possible will become pregnant in that time. I even give up my nights with the emperor in order to give the other girls more chances.

Two months later, three more girls are pregnant.

It becomes exhausting, celebrating and organizing and preparing for so many new babies. The children will all need wetnurses and nannies and eventually their own palaces and staff. I'm so busy and so happy, I hardly have time to even worry about Lihua. I try my best to put her out of my mind and work on being the best empress I can be.

⌒

I'm working late, going over the accounts with Fiyanggu to try and allocate more money to all the pregnant consorts while still keeping our expenses as low as possible.

"We can always cut back on their food," Fiyanggu says. "They don't eat most of what they are given anyway."

"But the leftovers go to their servants," I say. "I don't want to take food from them."

"What about their silk allocation?" Fiyanggu asks.

"No," I say. "Winter is coming, so they will need more silk than usual to sew warmer clothes." I sit back in my chair and rub my forehead.

"You should rest, Your Majesty," Fiyanggu says. "It is the middle of the night."

"Is it so late?" I ask, looking at the window and seeing only darkness outside. "I'm sorry. You should go. I know you must get up early. I'll work on this."

"No, Your Majesty," Fiyanggu says. "I can't sleep while you work. I'd never get any rest. The guilt would eat me up."

"But we can't make good decisions if we are both tired," I say.

"It's my responsibility—"

I'm thankful when there is a knock at the door to stop our bickering.

"I'm sorry, Your Majesty," Nuwa says, entering the room. "But the dowager empress has requested your presence."

"In the morning?" I ask.

"No," she says. "Now."

"What? Why?"

"I don't know," she says. "I only know that one of her maids says that she wants to see you immediately."

I can't imagine what Fenfeng would need to see me for so urgently. We barely speak, especially lately since I've been so busy. But I suppose that is even more reason to go and see what she needs. It must be important for her to summon me, especially so late at night.

"Fine," I say. "Summon a sedan chair and help me dress."

I had only been wearing clothes fit for staying at home and working, but now I step into a pair of pot-bottom shoes and a nicer outer robe. Nuwa styles my hair nicely, but I don't bother with a headdress. As soon as I am presentable, I go to the waiting sedan chair.

"You can stay here," I tell Nuwa. "It's late and I'm sure I won't be out long."

As the men carry the chair, rocking me slowly from side to side, I start to feel drowsy and have to prop my head up to keep from falling asleep. I should have checked the time. How late is it? Why is Fenfeng summoning me so late? It can't be good news. Perhaps I should have brought Nuwa with me.

The chair stops abruptly, and I realize I must have been dozing. One of the men helps me step out of the chair, and her guards bow to me as I pass through the gate. The entire

Forbidden City is quiet at such a late time, but Fenfeng's palace seems especially quiet. The few lights that are burning are dim. None of her servants come out to greet me, nor do I hear any shuffling about. Since Fenfeng summoned me, I expected to be welcomed properly. But it is as if the whole palace is asleep.

I consider leaving and coming back in the morning when I hear...something. A sound. A yelp? A scuffle? I can't be sure, but it sets the hairs on the back of my neck on edge.

I step into Fenfeng's palace and call out softly, "Hello? Is anyone here? Anyone awake?"

I hear a whimper, like someone crying, so I walk toward it. Still, other than the noise, the palace is quiet. Where is everyone?

I turn a corner and open my mouth to scream, but nothing comes out. A woman is stumbling toward me. She is wearing a white sleeping gown and her long, dark hair falls around her shoulders. For a brief moment, I think it is the ghost woman, returned to haunt me. But then, I realize that it is Fenfeng. I've never seen her so unkempt, but then I realize she must have been prepared for sleeping. Then why did she summon me?

She lets out a moan of pain and leans against the wall with one hand. I then see the knife sticking out of her chest and the red blood dripping down the front of her white shift. I run to her and she leans against me.

"Fenfeng! What has happened?"

She coughs up blood and I feel her stumble. "He-he-help me."

I lay her on the ground and she reaches for the knife. I pull it out and then use the voluminous cloth of her sleeping gown to staunch the wound.

"Who did this to you?" I ask her.

"Don...don...don't trust her," Fenfeng says, blood seeping from the side of her mouth. She reaches up and grabs my collar with a bloody hand. "She will kill us all..."

"Who?" I ask as Fenfeng loses strength and falls back to the ground. "Fenfeng! Who?"

I hear a scream from behind me and look back to see Lihua standing there.

"Hurry!" I say. "Get help!"

"The empress is at it again!" Lihua yells. "The empress has killed the dowager!"

Suddenly, everything becomes clear to me. Fenfeng never summoned me here, Lihua did! Lihua has killed Fenfeng and wants me to take the blame! But I don't let her, not this time. Not like she did when she claimed I was trying to hurt her baby. I won't let her get away with it.

I jump to my feet and charge after her. Lihua screams and turns and runs far more quickly than I do. I realize she's wearing slippers. I kick off my pot-bottom shoes and continue chasing after her in my bare feet, but she reaches the door before I do.

When I exit the palace and enter the courtyard, I have to hold my hand up to shield my eyes from so much light. There are a dozen guards present and countless servants, many of them holding torches, making it appear as bright as day.

From somewhere in the crowd, I hear that familiar voice. "Stop her! She's trying to kill me!"

25

I feel a sudden rush of rage that Lihua would be accusing me of trying to hurt someone again. I take a step down from Fenfeng's palace, heading toward Lihua's voice, but all of the guards take a step toward me, their weapons drawn. Swords and spears and even a few guns are leveled at me, and the men holding them look afraid.

"How dare you!" I say, taking a stomping step toward the guards. They all jump back, but still they hold their weapons firm. Are they really going to try and physically stop me? Try to kill me? For Lihua? The guards' threats do nothing to calm my anger. In fact, it only enrages me further.

"Get out of here!" I tell the guards. I can tell that they are sweating, even though the night is cold. "You have no authority here in the inner court," I say. "Get out, now, or I will have all of you arrested and executed for treason!"

It's not fair, I know. They are tasked with keeping the emperor's women safe. But they are also under my command. What are they to do? Several of them lower their weapons, others hold them shakily.

"What are you doing?" Lihua asks. "She killed the dowager empress! Stop her!"

"Shut your mouth!" I order, pointing in the direction of the voice with the bloody blade still in my hand.

Lihua screams. "Oh! Save me! Help me! She's gone completely mad!"

"What is going on here?"

Everyone in the courtyard drops to their knees at the emperor's voice. Honghui looks at me, and all the anger and strength I felt rushes out of me when our eyes meet. His jaw drops and his eyes go big.

"Daiyu," Honghui says. "What have you done?"

I drop the dagger and it clatters to the ground. "Nothing," I say. "I've done nothing." I take a step toward him, but he holds out a hand to stop me.

"Where is the dowager empress?" he asks.

I shake my head as my eyes well with tears. I'm not sure why. I didn't like the woman. I'm certain that she was behind the assassination attempt on Empress Caihong. I'm sure that Lady An died because of her treachery. Perhaps I am not crying for her, but for myself. Fenfeng is dead, and I will surely get the blame. Everyone has seen me with the bloody knife. I look down and see that the front of my gown is soaked with blood. It must have happened as Fenfeng fell into my arms.

"She is dead, Your Majesty," I say, tears running down my cheeks.

"Why, Daiyu?" Honghui asks, his own eyes rimming with red as he tries to control his emotions. "Why did you do it?"

"I didn't!" I say. "She summoned me to her palace and when I arrived, someone had stabbed her."

Honghui's eyes flit to the knife on the ground. "You stabbed her."

"No!" I say.

"Then who?" he asks.

I open my mouth to accuse Lihua, but the words die in my throat. I believe it was Lihua, but I didn't actually see her do it. I suppose one of her servants could have done it on her behalf. Still, I'm sure Lihua is responsible. But I have no proof. If I blame her without evidence, Honghui might just take it as another example of my jealousy. Of my jealousy driving me crazy. But I can't let him think that I really am the person who did this terrible thing.

"It was Liling," I say. "She was there when I found Fenfeng."

Honghui looks at Lihua, who I can see better now that many of the guards have lowered their torches. Honghui grabs Lihua by the arm, dragging her to her feet. "Is this true? Did you do this?"

"No!" Lihua cries. "I loved her majesty! I was her lady-in-waiting. That is why I was here. I was attending my lady.

"I was in the next room, preparing tea, when I heard the empress arrive. She and Fenfeng argued, but I could not hear the exact words. Then, there was a scream. When I went to see what was wrong, I saw the empress kneeling over the dowager, the knife in the empress's hand."

"Lies!" I cry in desperation. "All lies! Fenfeng was already dying when I arrived!"

"Then why was the knife in your hand?" Honghui asked me.

I look down at my bloody hands and the knife on the

ground at my feet. "I...I...I don't know. I was trying to save her."

"Save her?" Lihua asks. "Everyone knows you hated the dowager."

"I didn't want her to die," I say. "I never hurt her."

"Enough!" Honghui snaps. Then he takes a step toward me. "Daiyu, something is terribly wrong with you."

"No," I say, taking a step back. "You can't possibly think I did this."

"I don't know what to think anymore," he says. "But ever since Liling became pregnant, you haven't been yourself. You haven't been...right."

Tears run down my cheeks at his words. "I've done *everything* right. You will soon have three more children because of me! I am a good wife and a good empress."

Honghui runs his hand over his mouth, and I can tell he is torn about what to do. Someone killed Fenfeng; *someone* will have to answer for that. And I'm the only person with blood on my hands.

"I'm sorry," Honghui says. "But I can't take that risk."

"What risk?" I ask. "Do you think I'm going to kill someone else?"

"I don't know," he says. "I need time to think." At that, he motions the guards forward. "Take the empress to the Cold Palace and lock the door."

"No!" I scream. I run toward Honghui and fall to the ground at his feet. "Please, please don't send me there!"

"It's for your own good, Daiyu," he says, taking a step back from me. "You'll be safe there."

"I'll die there!" I say.

He ignores my pleas as two guards grab my arms and pull me up to my feet, dragging me toward the gate of Fenfeng's palace.

"Don't send me there, Honghui!" I cry out after him even after he is gone from my sight. "Please, help me!" I try to pull away from the guards, but they are much too strong for me.

"Your Majesty!" I see Nuwa and Yanmei huddled together, watching in horror as I am dragged past them.

"Help me!" I call to them. "I didn't do it! It was Liling! It was Liling!"

I kick and scream the whole way to the Cold Palace. At the doors, the guards loosen their grip. Did they expect me to just walk inside? I push one of the guards away and kick the leg of the other one as I try to run away, but they quickly catch up with me and drag me back. This time, they toss me through the doors, causing me to fall forward on my knees in the main room of the Cold Palace. I get to my feet and try to rush the door, but I'm much too slow and the door is shut and barred. I bang on the door with my weak fists. I know I can't break out, but I refuse to be locked away without a fight.

"I didn't do it!" I yell. "You'll learn the truth. You'll see. She'll kill you all before she is done."

Through a small gap in the door, I can see the guards turn their backs on me. I slap the door one more time for good measure before turning to survey my situation.

Ever since Lady An's death, the Cold Palace has sat empty, but I never dared to approach it to see the inside. But now, I can see that it looks just as old and weathered on the inside as it does on the outside. The Cold Palace is a very small palace, little more than one large, open room. There are a few scattered rugs on the floor, but not enough to cover all of it. There are some chairs and tables, but they are splintered and broken. I doubt I could even sit on one without toppling over. There is a wooden bed frame to one side of the room with a tattered blanket on top of it. It's not even a kang for warmth.

I suddenly realize how cold it is in the room. I let out a shuddering breath and tuck my hands under my armpits. As I exhale, fog dances lightly in front of my face. It is not yet deep winter, it is not snowing yet, but it is still quite cold at night. I bitterly realize that I am no longer accustomed to sleeping without heat and plenty of blankets.

I notice that there is an old brazier sitting on the floor in the middle of the room. It is not even on a stand. I kneel down next to it and realize it is full of fresh coal and hay. Sat next to the brazier, I see a bit of flint and steel. It dawns on me that past ladies who were locked in here did not know how to start a fire on their own. Thankfully, how to start a fire is something that comes back to me easily. I arrange the hay in the middle of the brazier and surround it with the coal. After tapping the flint and steel together a couple of times, the hay alights. I move the coals over the fire, and soon the coal is burning hot and bright.

I let out a sigh of relief as I warm my hands over the glowing coals. I lean back and take a couple of calming breaths. As I stretch my neck, though, I look up, and see the tattered remains of a white scarf blowing gently in the warm breeze that wafts up from the brazier. I let out a cry and scoot away as far as I can, coming to rest against the door.

There are ghosts here.

Is that the remnant of the same scarf Lady An used to hang herself? Or some other poor, unfortunate lady who was sent here to carry out her own execution?

I pull my knees to my chest and rest my forehead on them as despair takes over. I'm going to die in here.

26

A light tapping sound on the door wakes me. I'm not sure how I managed to fall asleep in this dismal place. The boards on the bed were so warped and cracked, it was more comfortable to lie on the floor. Besides, the bed was too far from the brazier to get any warmth, so I laid the ratty blanket beside the brazier and wrapped myself up, leaving only my face exposed. All through the night, the old building creaked and moaned. Shadows danced in the light of the brazier, and I heard scurrying and scratching from mice in the walls. I didn't see any ghosts, but I felt their presence. A heavy sadness permeated the air and seemed to crush me with the weight of it.

At first, I think I've imagined the tapping sound. But after I come out of the fog of sleep, I realize the sound is real. I sit up quickly and take a deep breath, which makes me sneeze as I disturb the dust that has settled around me overnight. I jump to my feet and rush to the door, peeking through the cracked wood.

"Nuwa?" I ask hopefully. I should have known better.

"No," Lihua says a little too cheerfully. "It's me."

"What do you want?" I ask.

"I thought you must be hungry," she says, and I see that she is carrying a tray with a teapot, teacup, and a bowl of steaming porridge. My mouth waters and my stomach growls, but I don't want to take anything from the woman who accused me of murder and had me locked in this place.

"I don't want anything from you," I say even though I know it is stupid. It wouldn't do for me to die in here of starvation, but I can't stop myself. Besides, what if the food is poisoned? She stabbed Fenfeng with her own bare hands. Poisoning me must be so easy compared to that.

Lihua tuts her tongue a few times and places the tray on the ground outside the door. "Well, if you change your mind, I'm sure the guards will give it to you." I notice that the guards have stepped far enough away that they most likely cannot hear what we are saying.

"Why did you do it?" I ask her, keeping my voice low. "Why did you kill Fenfeng?"

"I didn't," she says confidently. "You did."

"Stop it," I hiss at her. "Honghui isn't here to hear your lies. Tell me the truth. What did I do to you? You have everything you could ever want."

"Not everything," Lihua says. She leans in close. "I'm not empress yet."

I scoff. "Why would you want to be empress? It's a difficult, thankless job. If I could, I'd give you the position."

"Exactly!" Lihua says. "You don't want what you have, but you can't give it to me either. The only way I can climb any higher is if you are dead. That's how you got the position, isn't it?"

"I didn't kill to get it," I say. "I wish with every ounce of my being that Caihong was still here."

She waves my words away as if they mean nothing. "It doesn't matter. We can't change the past."

"But why kill Fenfeng?" I ask. "She liked you, didn't she? She would have helped you plot against me if you'd asked her. She hated me."

Lihua shrugs. "I couldn't get close enough to kill you. After she took me into her household, I couldn't make your tea anymore."

I feel sick suddenly at the idea that she had already been poisoning me with the tea. "Did...did you poison my tea?"

"Yes," she says, "but not in the way you think. If I'd killed you back then, Yanmei would have been made empress, don't you think?"

"I don't know," I say.

"I couldn't kill you until my position was so high, it was guaranteed that I would be the next empress. So, I just gave you something to stop your monthly bleed so you would think you were pregnant. That way Honghui would have to take other women into his bed."

"You made me think I was pregnant so that Honghui couldn't sleep with me anymore," I say, feeling so stupid. So used. Once again, I feel a pang of loss for the baby that never existed. "But how did you know you would get pregnant?"

"I didn't," she says. "I just had to pray."

I scoff. "You would never leave something like that up to chance. It had to do with the ghost woman, didn't it?"

"You're catching on," she says. "I learned a lot from my mother before she died. I sent my servants out into the Peking streets to find a pregnant girl that looked like me. After all, Mother found you. There had to be more poor, pitiful street people out there willing to hand over their child for a price. Your parents sold you easily enough."

"I *chose* to come here," I say, slapping the door. "My parents never would have sold me."

She shrugs. "Believe what you want."

"But why did it matter if she looked like you?" I ask.

"Well, there was no chance the child was going to look like Honghui, so it needed to look like my child."

I sigh at my own stupidity. Of course, it made perfect sense. "But you didn't know she'd have a boy."

"True," Lihua says. "I figured if the baby were a girl, Honghui would at least see my potential and take me back to his bed again and again in an attempt to get a son. I could just do it over and over again until I had a son. But at least I don't need to go through all that again."

"Did you have to kill the poor woman?" I say. "She did what you asked. Surely she would have kept your secret."

"I couldn't know that," Lihua says. "Poor people have such shifting loyalties. They will go to whoever gives them the most money without a second thought."

"So, what happens now?" I ask. "You know I'm not going to let you poison me."

"It would be in your best interest if you did," she says. "It's only a matter of time before Honghui sends you a white scarf."

I feel like crumpling into myself at her words. I don't want to believe her. Surely Honghui would not think so poorly of me. But I'm in here while Lihua is out there feeding him more and more lies, poisoning his mind against me.

"I won't do it," I tell her, forcing my fears to the side for the moment. I can't let Lihua think she's beaten me. "I'll never admit guilt by taking my own life."

"Then you'll probably starve," Lihua says easily. "I don't think Honghui has it in himself to have you executed. He really is smitten with you, the poor idiot. You should teach me how you managed to get him to fall in love with you."

"You could start by not being a murdering monster," I say.

Lihua laughs. "Well, that's not going to happen."

"Your mother would be horrified at what you've done," I say, and Lihua's face drops for a moment. "She sacrificed everything to keep you out of here. To give you a different life."

"Mother was selfish," she spits. Her anger surprises me. "She thought so very little of me. She thought I would be a lowly, insignificant concubine for the rest of my life. She had no idea how high I could climb. If she had believed in me for even a moment, she never would have stood in my way."

"Did you kill her too?" I ask. "Is that how she died? She never would have let you come here if she had lived."

"You know," Lihua says thoughtfully, "you're not as stupid as I thought you were."

"That means a lot coming from you," I say. She blinks. I don't think she meant her words to be a compliment. She screws up her face and lifts her chin.

"I'll keep bringing food to you," she says. "I'm sure you'll see reason soon enough." She spins around on her pot-bottom shoes and walks away from me quickly, as if to escape some biting retort I might shoot at her. I wish I had one, but I don't.

I let out a sigh and lean against the door. My stomach growls again. "Stop it," I whisper. "We've gone hungry before. You're just spoiled." I needed to get used to being hungry again. I don't know for sure how long it takes for someone to actually die of starvation. I myself never went more than a day or two completely without food. I would often give up meals for my younger siblings, but I had to eat eventually. But I know some of our neighbors fared worse. Occasionally, we would hear rumors of someone starving and not being found for days or weeks. Usually an old and forgotten relative of people who had gone to find work at the docks or in another part of the city. I wondered how long it would take Honghui to forget me.

I picked at the bottom of a window frame. The wood was rotten and flaked away easily. I pulled at it a little more forcefully with the tips of my fingers, wondering if it would give way enough for me to eventually open the window, but I cried out in pain as a splinter stuck one of my fingers, causing it to bleed. I sucked on the finger and used my teeth to pull the splinter out. I sighed in frustration.

"What do you mean?" I heard a woman's voice say loudly from the front of the palace. The guards replied, but I couldn't make out their words. "That's ridiculous!" the woman went on. I went to the door and peeked through the crack. My heart swells when I see Yanmei there holding a tray of food.

"I am the empress's lady, not Liling," Yanmei is saying. My mouth waters at the sight of the bowls of food she is carrying on a tray. Still, the guards hold up their hands, keeping her from approaching the door. I am about to yell out, to order them to let her pass, when I hear a scratching sound coming from the back of the room. At first, I think it is a rat, or maybe a bird, and ignore it, but the scratching grows louder. I walk toward the window, scanning the room for any errant vermin, and hear a whispered voice.

"Daiyu?"

"Dongmei!" I run to the window and peek through a crack before nearly bursting into tears at the sight of the little girl. "Oh, my darling! What are you doing here?"

"I'm here to help you," she says.

I choke out a laugh as the tears start to fall. "You sweet, kind child. Please, don't worry about me. Everything will be fine. I promise."

"How?" she asks, and I am speechless.

"What do you mean?" I manage to ask.

"How will everything be fine?"

"I...I don't know," I have to admit.

"Then listen to me," she says, and I'm dumbfounded. This is more than she has said to me in the whole time since my return to the Forbidden City. "If I can get you out of the Cold Palace, can you get out of the Forbidden City?"

I think back to the time I climbed a tree to scale the wall of the Forbidden City in a foolish attempt to find my family. It seemed so long ago now.

"Yes," I say. "I think so." I haven't checked to see if the tree is still there, if its limbs are still low enough for me to reach. I've had no reason to want to leave since I had wanted to return this time. But I have to hope everything is as it was before.

"Okay," she says. "I'll see what I can do." She starts to turn away.

"Wait," I say. "Why are you doing this? I thought you hated me."

"I don't hate you," she says, and her face looks hurt. My heart swells.

"I did write to you," I tell her. "Every week. I missed you so much."

"I know," she says, and she reaches into her sleeve. To

my surprise, she pulls out a letter that I recognize as one I sent her from the Temple of Grief.

"Where did you get that?" I ask.

"Fiyanggu gave me all your letters," she says. "In secret. Jiangfei doesn't even know. I couldn't risk Grandmother—" Her voice catches for a moment. "I couldn't risk Grandmother finding out. She would have been furious."

"Then...then why were you so angry with me?" I ask.

"You still left me!" she says, stomping her foot and shoving the letter back into her sleeve.

"Okay, okay," I say, trying to calm her down and shush her. "I understand."

Dongmei wipes at her cheeks with her sleeve. "I didn't know if you would stay this time or not. And I guess you won't. But I'd rather you run away again than die."

"Dongmei..." I run my fingers over the crack in the door. How I wish to hold her hand, or at least touch her face. But I can't. "I'm sorry. I'm so sorry for everything."

"Me too," Dongmei says.

"Go on, now!" I hear one of guards yell, and Dongmei hears it too.

"I have to go," she says.

"I love you!" I call out to her.

"I love you too, Mama," she says. "I'll get you out of there somehow." Then, she runs off around the side of the building and out of sight.

"Mama..." I whisper as I sink down to the floor. Her words lift my soul and stab my heart. I wish I didn't have to leave her or Jiangfei again. It hurts so much to leave them. But I am also reminded about how much I miss my own mother. She surely must miss me as well.

I remember Tao Fashi at the Temple of Grief. She once asked me what I really wanted. Did I want to return to the

Forbidden City, or did I want to find my family. I didn't hesitate to say that I wanted to find my parents. Now, it seems that I might finally have that chance. I don't know how Dongmei plans to get me out of the Cold Palace, but if she does, I will find my way home.

I will find my mother.

27

The little bit of hope I had been feeling starts to fade as day turns to night. What can Dongmei do to help me? I admire her strength, but she's just a little girl. Of course, she's not alone. Yanmei was obviously distracting the guards so that they would not hear her talking to me. Dongmei, Yanmei, Nuwa, Jinhai. Individually, they are all smart, clever people. Together, surely they will be able to come up with some sort of plan to help me.

"Why are you slacking?" I hear someone back in a gruff voice. When I peek out the door, I have to stifle a gasp when I see Jinhai in a guard's uniform.

"What do you mean?" one of the guards asks.

"You look like you are about to fall asleep on the job," Jinhai says.

"No, sir!" the guard says. Jinhai and the man argue back and forth for a minute, but I lose the conversation when I hear tapping on the back window. I rush over and about faint when I see Honghui standing there.

"What...what are you doing here?" I ask. Honghui holds a finger to his lips as he uses a metal bar to pry loose the plank that is holding the window shut. I hear Jinhai's voice rising louder, and the guards replying in kind. Honghui opens the shudders and helps me climb through. He then closes the shudder and replaces the plank as best he can. He then grabs my hand and we sneak through the bushes of the garden around the Cold Palace, snaking our way through the gardens and down the paths of the inner court until we reach an empty building, one that I remember having secret trysts in with Honghui when I was just a concubine to Emperor Guozhi.

"What's going on?" I whisper as he closes the door.

"I'm breaking you out, you little fool," he says. "Dongmei says you know how to get out of the Forbidden City on your own."

"Dongmei? What? How? Why?" I'm so confused.

"Because I love you," he says. "Isn't that obvious?"

"Then why not just release me?" I ask.

"I can't," he says, shaking his head in dismay. "Someone killed the dowager empress. Someone has to be held accountable."

"Then arrest Liling," I say. "She is the one who did it."

"I don't have any evidence," he says. "And you made a big show in front of the servants and guards, waving that bloody knife around."

I have to nod at that. "I admit that I was not exactly in the best frame of mind at that moment. But neither would you have been if you had been the one to find a woman dying in your arms."

"I'm not here to argue," he says. "I'm here to save your life."

"What do you mean?" I ask.

Honghui goes to a dark corner of the room and pulls out a bag, handing it to me. I open it and pull out dark servant clothes. "Put them on, then I will help you get out of here."

"Then what?" I ask.

"I don't know," he says. He opens the door a crack and peeks out into the dark night as I change my clothes. When I'm done, my mind feels transported back to the night I escaped from the Forbidden City all on my own. Suddenly, I'm afraid. I'm not the same person I was back then. I don't want to leave. I have nowhere to go. Back then, I still harbored hope that my family would be in our old home waiting for me. Now, I know they are not there. I can't go back to Tao Fashi at the Temple of Grief. This time when I leave the Forbidden City, I will be completely alone.

"I can't do this," I say, my voice small and shaky.

"What are you talking about?" Honghui asks me.

"Where am I to go?" I ask. "What will I do?"

Honghui closes the door and walks over to me, taking my hands in his and kissing my forehead. I close my eyes and try not to cry.

"You are the bravest, most resilient woman I know," Honghui says. "Have we not always found our way back to each other?"

I shake my head. "Everything is different now. You are emperor. Once I leave here, I'll be a wanted woman. A woman accused of murder. By running away, everyone will think I really am guilty."

"Then we must prove your innocence," he says. "Somehow we will prove that you didn't do this thing. And better yet, we will find proof that Liling really is the person who killed Fenfeng."

"But how?" I ask.

"I don't know!" Honghui says in frustration, his own eyes growing glassy. "But we have to try."

I have no faith that once I climb over the great red walls of the Forbidden City that I will ever be able to return to this place, but still, I nod. Honghui still has hope—however faint—that we will be together again, and I can't take that from him.

"Yes," I say. "Yes, of course. All we can do is try. We can't let her get away with what she's done."

"Exactly," he says. He reaches into his sleeve and hands me a small purse. "Some money to help you." I take the purse and slip it into a pocket in my own sleeve.

"Now, how do we get you out of here?" Honghui asks.

"Behind the palace I lived in when I first arrived at the Forbidden City as a concubine there was a large, old tree. It reaches up taller than the outer wall, but it had branches low enough for me to reach."

Honghui nods thoughtfully. "You climbed the tree and went over the wall and then...what? Dropped thirty feet to the ground on the other side?"

I shrug as I remember the terrifying fall and the pain as I landed.

"I can't believe you didn't die," Honghui says, "or at least break something."

"I didn't think it through," I say. "All I wanted was to get out."

"But you came back," Honghui says. "Why?"

"I didn't have anywhere else to go," I say.

"Your mother—"

"My family was gone," I say. His mouth drops open. I'm tired of lying. This could be the last time I see Honghui, and I don't want to leave without telling him the truth. "I'm not Ula-Nara Lihua. I never was. I was—" I bite my tongue and curse myself that I still can't bring myself to tell him that I'm Han Chinese. That I'm not Manchu.

"My family was poor, so poor we often didn't have enough food to eat. Lihua's mother, Mingxia, offered my family money if I took her daughter's place at the selection for Guozhi's consorts. My parents didn't want to accept, but I couldn't let them go hungry. My littlest sister was only a baby, and she was surely going to die if I didn't take the money. I took Lihua's place.

"I never thought I would be selected. I thought I would just attend the ceremony and then be sent home. When I ended up being selected, I panicked. I was miserable. So, I escaped. But when I got to our old home, my family was gone. I have no idea where they went or what happened to them."

Honghui lets out an exhale and rubs his forehead. "You're not Lihua. Then who are you?"

"My name is Daiyu," I say.

Honghui nods. "Of course." Still, he looks overwhelmed as he tries to process all I've told him. He's not looking at me.

"I'm sorry," I say. "I wanted to tell you so many times. I should have told you before I agreed to marry you. But I was afraid. If anyone ever found out that I had lied, that I'd deceived the emperor, I could have been put to death. I'm sorry."

"That's why it is so important to you to send money to the poor," he says slowly. "You know what being poor is like."

"Yes," I say simply.

"I can't imagine what your life must have been like," Honghui says. "I suppose you must have been very desperate to take such a risk."

"I was," I say. "But that's no excuse. I shouldn't have lied...at least, not to you."

"I understand why you did," Honghui says. He looks at me and cups my face, placing his forehead against mine. "Thank you for finally trusting me."

My heart breaks at his words and I grunt in frustration, pulling away from him. "I'm not Manchu!"

Confusion passes over Honghui's face. "What?" he asks slowly.

"I'm not Manchu," I say. "I'm Han."

Honghui takes a step back as he runs his hand over his face. "You're...not Manchu?"

"No," I say, shaking my head. "I'm not."

"Daiyu...Daiyu..." He seems to be having problems putting words together, and I don't blame him. "This can't... I don't... Do you know what you've done?"

"I do now," I say. "I didn't at the time. Like I said, I never thought I'd be chosen."

"You're the empress!" he says. "The empress of the Qing Dynasty. The *Manchu* Dynasty. How...how could you do this?"

"I never wanted to be empress!" I say, but then I catch myself. "At least, not for Guozhi. I tried to hide among the women of the harem. To be invisible."

"Daiyu," Honghui says, "you should know that you could never be invisible. You shine like a star even on the brightest of days."

I shake my head. "I don't know how it happened. But when Guozhi banished me, I thought it was over. I thought I'd never see you again. But then you came for me. You asked me to be your wife. I knew it was stupid, that it was dangerous, but I couldn't say no. I loved you so much."

"I loved you too," Honghui says. "I still love you." He runs his hand through my hair and then cups my head, pulling me closer for a kiss. I don't want to let him go, but I know I must.

"Do you still want me to leave?" I ask. "If I do, we might not ever see each other again."

"We will be together again," he says. "I don't know how, but I promise that we will be."

I nod, unable to speak. I don't know how he can be so optimistic.

"Who is Liling?" he asks suddenly.

"What?"

"What does Liling have to do with you?" he asks. "Why does she hate you so much?"

"Oh," I say. "She is the real Lihua. She is the girl whose place I took. Her mother didn't want to lose her to the emperor."

"Then what is she doing here?" he asks.

I shrug. "She says that her mother has died and she resents me for taking what she saw as her rightful place as empress."

"So, now that she has my son," Honghui says, "she wants you dead so she can take your place."

I have to smile a little at just how clever Honghui is. "Yes."

"Well, that's not going to happen," he says. "I'm going to do whatever it takes to get you back."

"Don't tell her that," I say. "She's dangerous. Desperate. We have to do this right."

"Of course. I have my most trusted men looking into the dowager's death. Hopefully they will find something we can use to prove your innocence. Maybe while you are on the outside, you can learn something that will help."

"Like what?" I ask.

"I don't know," he says. "But you know the truth about her. You could find something."

"I'll try," I say, though I don't hold out any hope.

From the center of the Forbidden City, a large gong is struck, indicating the time. It is still the middle of the night, but we should not waste any more time. I need to be well away from here before the sun rises.

"Come," Honghui says, taking my hand. "I can't let you escape from this place just to fall to your death. I know another way out."

"Is it the door you used the night we met?" I ask.

Even in the darkness, I can see his face flush bright red. "Yes," he says. He pauses and I raise my eyebrow at him. I bared my soul, after all. Now, he can return the favor.

"You want to know why I was sneaking out that night we met," he says. I say nothing. "You already know, don't you?" I stay quiet. "Fine. I had been seeing Lady An that night. I hadn't slept with her in a very long time, but I cared for her and still called on her on occasion. Dongmei...Dongmei is our daughter."

"Why didn't you try to save her?" I ask.

"How dare you?" he asks, pulling his hand away from me. "What makes you think I didn't? I spoke to my brother at length about her. He knew that Dongmei was my daughter, but he wasn't angry about it since, at that time, he had no children. He was afraid that he was unable to have children. Dongmei allowed him to save face among the nobles. When Jiangfei was born, though, he knew he was the father. I never would have touched Caihong. But since we then knew that Guozhi was capable of having children of his own, he resented Lady An and me for what we had done. I think that by ordering Lady An to kill herself, Guozhi felt he was getting revenge on me as well."

"I'm sorry," I say. "Her death must have hurt you very much."

"I didn't love her," Honghui is a little too quick to say. "I was young and stupid and took advantage of her loneliness. But I am so very sorry that Dongmei lost her mother. Things were different with you—"

"Shh." I place my fingers over his mouth to stop him from trying to justify his past. "You don't have to explain yourself to me."

Honghui kisses the tips of my fingers and then holds my hand to his chest. "When we are together again, we both have a lot to atone for."

"We will," I say, "when we are together again."

He presses his lips together and nods. "Come on. Let's get you out of here."

He leads me out of the building and through the many winding paths and gardens of the inner court. When we get to the small door, there is a single guard standing watch. Honghui motions for me to stay hidden while he approaches the guard. I thought that he would talk to the man, order him to leave, or maybe bribe him to walk away. I gasp when I see Honghui sneak up behind the man and wrap his arms around the man's neck. The man struggles to fight back and call for help, but he was so caught off guard, he can do nothing. A moment later, Honghui lays the unconscious guard on the ground and motions for me to join him.

"Is he dead?" I ask as Honghui removes the gate key from the guard's belt.

"Of course not," Honghui says, fiddling with the lock. "He'll wake up soon."

The lock clicks and the door lets out a low groan as it is

pulled open. I take a deep breath before I step through. Honghui grabs my hand.

"You will come back," Honghui says. "I know you will."

I'm not sure if he is trying to reassure me or himself, but I squeeze his hand and nod. "I will. I promise."

He kisses me one more time, then he practically pushes me out the door and into the dark night on the other side of the great red wall. Suddenly alone, I look left and right. I don't see any guards, so I rush across the wide road and slip down a narrow hutong to hide.

28

I crouch down behind a cart and watch as a guard walks past the small door in the great red wall. He raises his hand to his mouth as he yawns. I sigh with relief at the knowledge that I had not been seen. But what would I do now? The moon was high in the sky. I knew of a couple of inns in the area, but even the innkeepers would be asleep at such a late hour. I feel a smile creep across my face at the idea of returning to my old home. I know my family won't be there, but just the idea of going "home" fills me with joy.

I walk quickly and quietly. It's not exactly safe to wander the hutongs alone at night, at least for a woman. I pass by a drunken man slumped against a wall who is singing a song from the opera *Peony in Love*. Well, I say singing, but it sounds more like a catfight. I stay on the opposite side of the street of a brothel, its red lanterns swaying in the breeze. The sounds of laughter float through the doors, but I can see a young woman standing by an upstairs window, tears streaking down her face. I linger to look at her face a little too long, and she sees me watching. When our eyes meet, I quickly tear them away and practically run to the next block. That woman could have been me. I pray it is not what happened to my sisters. Surely my father did better by them than that after the sacrifice I made.

I pass by the market where I used to buy rice and pork to feed my family. I have to plug my nose at the smells of rancid meat and animal feces. I don't remember the market stinking so badly when I lived here. I then realize that it isn't the market smell that has changed, but me. I haven't had to put up with a nasty, filthy market in years. I never even went to the kitchens when I lived in the Forbidden City. At the Temple of Grief, the kitchens were kept immaculately clean by the women assigned to work there, which I never was.

Finally, I come to the alley where our house was located. For some reason, my pace slows as I approach it. I know my family won't be there, but still there is a well of hope in my chest that maybe they will be. What if, for some reason, much like myself, they found themselves here once again. Back at the beginning. I feel excited at the prospect, but then terribly sad. If they ended up back here again, it would mean that they lost all the money they had earned from selling me. No, I have to hope that they are not here, no matter how much I long to see them.

I push lightly on the door, and it doesn't budge. I push a little harder, and the top of the door shudders, but the bottom doesn't, as if there is something at the bottom blocking it. I hear a low growl from behind me. I look over my shoulder and see a dog on a rope outside of a nearby house watching me. I have to be careful not to make too much noise. I don't want to set the dog to barking and wake the neighbors. I lean against the door and press my weight against it. The door begins to move, and there is a scraping sound as whatever was against the bottom of it is pushed across the floor. Finally, the door is open and moonlight streams into the large room.

"Huh? What?"

I gasp and then press my hand to my mouth as a person who was lying on the floor sits up. The dog starts barking and I hear a voice from another house yell.

"Shh!" I say as I step into the room and close the door behind me. I see that the door had been held closed by a large rock, but I leave the door open a crack to let some of the light in.

"What? Who are you?" the man says as he looks around in confusion. At first, I think he is just drowsy, but the way he wobbles, I think he must also be a bit drunk. His hair is long and matted, filthy. He hasn't shaved in who knows how long. His clothes are rags and his nails are practically claws.

"My name is Daiyu," I say, keeping my voice low. I hear another neighbor shout for the dog to shut up. "I used to live in this house."

"Daiyu..." the man says, his voice gravelly. He blinks and rubs his forehead. For a brief moment, my heart seizes at the idea that this man could be my father. But no. I shake my head and thank the gods that it isn't. But there is something familiar about him.

"Who are you?" I ask him.

He lets out a long breath as if trying to remember his own name. "Fa..." he finally says slowly. "Dong Fa."

"I remember you!" I say. He had been our neighbor for many years. He had several daughters around the same ages as my sisters. His wife and my mother would sometimes sit and embroider together. But in the days before I met Mingxia, he had completely run out of money and hope. He had sold his daughters to a brothel. In her grief, his wife had killed herself. The last time I saw him, he had been drinking away the money he'd received from selling his daughters in a public house down the road. He had been one of the reasons why I'd agreed to Mingxia's scheme. I didn't want my family to end up like his.

"Yes," the man says. "Daiyu... You're Old Hong's daughter, aren't you?"

I let out a small cry of joy at hearing my family name, my *real* family name, for the first time in years.

"Yes," I say. "My father was Hong Wen. Do you know what happened to him? Where are my mother and sisters?"

Dong Fa sits up and stretches, rubbing the back of his neck. "Why did you wake me? The only peace I get is when I sleep."

"I'm sorry," I say, sitting down across from him and crossing my legs. "I've come a long way and was hoping my family would still be here."

"I thought you married," Dong Fa says, clearing some phlegm and spitting it across the room. "What happened? Husband beat you?"

"No," I say, shaking my head. But I suppose I should have just said yes. I hardly want to tell this man my story, and he doesn't want to hear it. "He...he died," I settle on, which is at least partly the truth. My first husband did die after all.

"Death comes to us all," the man muses. "But not soon enough for some of us."

"The gods perhaps still have a plan for you," I say.

Dong Fa lets out a chuckle, but there is no humor in it. "So, you are looking for your family."

"Yes," I say. "Do you know what happened to them?"

"Your father said you'd married well," Dong Fa says. "That your husband had not demanded a dowry but had given your father a large bride price."

I nod slowly.

"I have to wonder how a girl from this neighborhood managed to find a husband such as that. Especially a girl like you with big feet."

I gulp and wait for him to continue. He must want something. Money, I suppose.

"My wife bound the feet of each of our daughters," Dong Fa goes on. "Oh, how they screamed in pain. You must have heard it, your house being so close to ours."

I nod again. I don't remember his daughters crying in pain specifically, but there were many nights when I couldn't sleep because of the screams coming from somewhere in the neighborhood as another girl was subject to that rite of passage that would help secure her future and, hopefully, that of her family.

"I thought that the death of our youngest daughter from infection was the worst pain I would ever experience as a father. But I couldn't have been more wrong. Seeing the fear on the faces of the other girls as I sold them to that madam was far worse. It's those faces that haunt me day and night. Those faces are why I long for eternal sleep."

I don't want to hear anymore. I reach into my sleeve and pull out a couple of coins. I lay them out on the floor between us.

"Please. Please, tell me where I can find my family."

Dong Fa takes the coins and slips them somewhere out of sight so quickly, it was practically a magic trick.

"There is a mountain north of here, Baiyun," he says. "They live in a village near there called Sitao. I hear he has a farm there and a big house."

"Really?" I ask, my heart racing. Hopefully that means my father has done well for himself since we parted ways.

The man shrugs. "I only know what he told me."

"When did you last speak to him?" I ask.

"I don't know. One day is like the next. He gave me this hole in the wall to live so I wouldn't freeze to death. I guess I shouldn't have accepted. Why should I want to prolong my life?"

"Maybe one day your daughters will return too," I say.

He's quiet for a while at that thought. "Maybe."

It seems we have nothing left to say to each other. I look back out the door, but the sun still has not started to rise.

"Can I stay here until morning?" I ask. "I'll travel to my father's village at first light."

"Do whatever you want," he says as he stands up, stretching his back. "I'm sure I can find somewhere to spend these coins."

"Good luck, Uncle," I say as he opens the door and steps out into the cold night. I can at least pay him that respect.

"And you," he says. "I hope you find them." He lets the door slam behind him and the dog starts barking again. "Ah, shut your mouth, you mangey mutt..." I hear him mutter as he wanders off down the road.

I know I won't get any sleep, but neither will I find a carriage heading out of town at this time of night. I lean against a wall and pull the ratty blanket over my big, flat feet, which are jittery with excitement. I'm so close to finding my family. I know I'll see them soon.

29

I ask around the next morning and find out there is a carriage that will leave from the square in front of the Forbidden City heading for Baiyuan Mountain. While I wait, I can't help but wander the streets a little, losing myself in memories. My mouth waters at the smell of steamed pork buns, buns I could rarely afford. The money Honghui gave me hangs heavy in my sleeve, and my stomach growls loudly. I buy one of the buns, and I eat it so quickly I forget to breathe between bites. I'm panting when I'm done, and I buy another one.

When I'm full, I wander a bit more and come upon a crowd watching the same opera troupe that was performing here years ago. And they are performing the same opera, *Drunken Beauty*. The young man playing the part of the concubine seems not to have aged a day, though that could be because of all the makeup he is wearing. This time when the dwarf and his monkey come around asking for donations, I put a coin in his cup.

I turn my head to see if the carriage has arrived, but instead, I see the old shoe seller, the one I had sold my shoes to in order to have enough money to buy food for my family. My heart clutches as the memory. Had I really been so poor it was better to go barefoot? I can hardly imagine it now. That was the last time I went to bed hungry.

I walk over toward the shoe seller's stall, not really looking at it, pretending that something else has my attention. I'm not sure why I'm approaching the stall. There is nothing but painful, sad memories here. But then I see them. The shoes I had sold. *My* shoes. The shoes that Mama had embroidered for me with delicate red flowers. Even from a distance, I can see the quality. Truly, Mama was a skilled artisan. Of all the fancy, beautiful, expensive shoes I have owned since, none were as detailed as the ones my mother embroidered for me.

"A pretty lady like you needs a pretty pair of shoes," the seller says. He reaches for a pair that is obviously new, never worn. I reach up and toy with my hair awkwardly. Do I really look like I can afford a new pair? I'm wearing the simple black clothes of a maid, my hair plaited down my back. I don't look like a lady. At least, I don't think I do. But as I watch the man practically falling over himself to sell to me, I realize that it must not be my clothes that give me away as a lady, but something else. Some unnamable quality that I now possess.

"Actually, I was wondering about that pair," I say, pointing toward my own shoes nestled among a dozen others.

"That one?" the seller asks, confused. "Why, the shoes you are wearing are better than those."

I look down at my simple, black maid shoes and realize he's right. Even the maids in the Forbidden City dress better than I did when I lived here. I just shrug.

"They are prettier," I say. "How much?"

"Hmm..." The seller picks up the shoes and rubs his chin. He must think I'm an easy target. He doesn't know that I know what he paid for the shoes, or that they have been sitting on his stall shelf for years. On one hand, it makes me kind of sad that the shoes have never sold. On the other hand, I am glad they are still here for me to buy.

The seller quotes me a price for the shoes three times what he paid me for them. I laugh.

"You said yourself that the shoes I'm wearing are better than those, yet you try to charge me so much?" I start to walk away.

"Okay, okay, Little Sister," the man says. He then quotes me a lower price. Still more than he paid me for them, but I understand that he is running a business, so I hand over the coins. I practically snatch the shoes out of his hands as he offers them to me. A moment ago, buying them had seemed more of a game. But now that I actually have them in my hands, the feel of them, the smell, the memories of watching my mother stitch them together in the light from the open door, all of it nearly drives me to tears.

"Say, you look familiar," the seller says as I start to walk away, cradling my precious purchase.

"I get that a lot," I say as a carriage pulls up and stops, sending plumes of dust into the air.

I pay the driver his fee and climb up to take a seat. Once I'm seated, I change my shoes, putting on the pretty black slippers with embroidered red flowers. Oddly, they are more comfortable than the other ones I'd been wearing, despite the supposed lower quality. I guess it's because I've worn these shoes before. They fit me like no other pair ever has.

Several more people climb into the carriage until we are all crammed together. I lean against the opposite door, thankful for the window and fresh air. I fidget with the maid's shoes in my hands and then realize how gross it is to be handling them after walking all over the place in them. But I don't have a bag to put them in. As the carriage starts to pull away, I shrug and toss the shoes out the window in the direction of the shoe seller. Hopefully he can make a couple of coins off them.

~

When I paid my fare, the driver had said Baiyuan mountain was half a day's ride north of Peking. It's mid-afternoon by the time the carriage stops and the driver tells me to get out. I see only a small collection of houses and a market with half a dozen sellers. Looking around in every direction, I see only wide-open space. I'm truly in the middle of nowhere. I ask around and find an old farmer willing to let me ride in the back of his donkey cart to Sitao Village. Not only that, he says he will drive right past my father's farm.

"You know Hong Wen?" I ask in shock.

"Everyone knows Old Hong," the man says with a laugh as he urges his donkey on with a weak tap from his whip. "The only thing he has more than money is daughters!" His laugh turns to a cough in the dry air.

Well, the remark about having lots of daughters certainly sounds like my father. But having lots of money? I know how much Mingxia paid for me. And she was supposed to give my family even more money after I was selected as a consort, but I don't know if she ever did. Still, the money Mingxia had given my father was a good sum, but not enough for my family to be counted as rich. If they lived simply, frugally, they could make the money last. But it sounds as if they didn't do that. If other people consider

Father rich, he must be living quite lavishly. I hope Father did not squander the money away and now sit only on a fortune of debt.

We amble along the road and I see a large rice paddy that is brown and fallow for the winter. Beyond it, I see a large manor house made of gray stones. On either side of the manor house are small, brown brick farmhouses.

"There," the farmer says, pulling his overworked donkey to a stop and pointing to the manor house. "Sitao Village."

I slid off the back of the cart, my heart beating rapidly. "And where does Old Hong live? One of the farmhouses?"

"What? No. There!" He points to the manor house again.

"You...you mean the big house?" I ask. "You can't be serious."

"Go on, see for yourself," the farmer says. Then he taps at his donkey again, leaving me behind without another word.

Leaving me alone on the road, I have no choice but to go into the village and ask around for my family. The man must have been mistaken, or joking. My father couldn't possibly afford a house such as this. It's so huge, it must have dozens of rooms, many servants.

The village is quite lively. I see a couple of kids guiding a herd of ducks to a pond. An old man is leading a couple of cows to a field to graze. A butcher is cutting up a fat hog. Some women are using a hand pump to fill buckets of water for washing and cooking.

From around the side of the large house, from down the road, I see a group of well-dressed young ladies. They all have on brightly colored robes, hair styled with pins and flowers, and beautifully embroidered shoes. Three of the girls obviously have bound feet, based on the careful way they sway as they walk. The fourth girl, though, is taller than the others and walks confidently on pot-bottom shoes. They all laugh and chatter as if they don't have a care in the world. If I weren't in the middle of the countryside, I would think they were imperial ladies.

I stop when I catch sight of the girl in the middle of the group. Her face is as familiar to me as my own. My throat squeezes so tightly, I can't speak. One of the other girls notices me and taps the lead girl on the shoulder. When our eyes meet, the girl stops and freezes, all the color draining from her face as if she's seen a ghost.

"Mingming," I finally choke out.

"Daiyu?" she asks, shaking her head in confusion.

I nod and stumble toward her, my arms outstretched. The other girls scatter as if they are afraid I carry some terrible disease, or that I might just get them dirty. But Mingming eagerly embraces me.

"Is it really you?" she asks.

"Yes!" I manage to say. "Yes, it's me."

"Mama and Baba will be so thrilled to see you."

I have to pull back to look at her face and make sure she isn't toying with me. "They are here? Really?"

"Of course," Mingming says. She points to the big manor house. "They are right inside."

"They really live here?"

Mingming looks at me, as if I am the one telling a joke, then she laughs. She tugs on my arm and leads me into the house. We step over the threshold and I have to look around in wonder at how beautiful the courtyard is.

"Ma! Ba!" Mingming calls out as she drops my hand and runs off. There is a large pond in the middle of the courtyard, and all around it are trimmed hedges and pretty flowers in pots. There is a second story to the house with a balcony that wraps all around the inside. At the far side of the courtyard, there is an elevated stage for opera or music performances. I'm so completely lost in the grandeur of it all, it's as if I'm awakened from a dream when I hear my name called.

"Daiyu!"

I turn around and see two elderly people I almost don't recognize, or don't want to recognize. How could my parents have aged so much in such a short period of time? But as they come toward me, their arms outstretched, none of that matters. We run to each other, and I fall into their arms.

"Daiyu! Daiyu!" they say over and over again.

"Are you really here?" my mother asks.

"Mama. Baba. I'm home."

30

That evening, I see all my sisters, even the youngest, who had been just an infant the last time I saw her. She had been so tiny, I thought she was going to either starve or freeze to death. Now, she's a healthy and rambunctious toddler.

"Her name is Daiyu," my mother tells me later as we sit outside under the stars, wrapped in brackets next to a warm fire. It's just the two of us, the girls having gone to bed and Baba working with his steward to go over some accounts.

"Daiyu?" I say as I sip a cup of hot tea.

"When you left, it was as if you had died," she explains. "We never thought we would see you again. So, since the baby didn't have a name, we thought it was a good way to honor your memory. Your sacrifice."

"I understand," I say. "I never thought I would see any of you again. There were many times I thought I *was* going to die. I thought for sure I was going to be caught. That I was going to be tried for treason and executed."

"But you weren't," Mama says. "You survived. And now you are here."

"Yes," I say. "I don't know this place, but I truly feel like I am home since I am with you."

"Are you here to stay?" she asks cautiously.

I shake my head. "I don't know."

She hesitates before asking, "Do you want to tell me how you came to be here?"

Finally and freely I tell her my story—every part of it. Even the parts I'm not proud of. Every word is like another rock falling from my shoulders. When I finish, Mama is quiet.

"I'm sorry," I say. "I'm sorry I've disappointed you."

"Disappointed?" Mama gasps. "How could you ever think that?"

"You were so quiet. I thought... I don't know. I thought maybe you were angry with me."

"Daiyu," she says, taking my hand and squeezing it. "You've been through so much, but you only ever did what you had to do to survive. I couldn't be prouder of you."

"Thank you," I say. I clear my throat to keep from crying again and motion toward the house. "It looks like you and Baba have done more than just survive. How did you end up here anyway?"

"Oh, it's a long story," she says.

"I tried to find you," I say. "I snuck out of the Forbidden City to see you, but you were gone."

"Yes, I'm sorry we weren't there," she says. "But by then, we knew you'd been selected and weren't coming back. Little Daiyu was starving and so cold. Your father finally decided there was no reason for us to stay there, so we left. We went to an inn and stayed together in a room with a real bed and a fireplace. The girls ate so much they got sick. But we were determined to not waste the money. Not waste the opportunity. Your father went to the docks, but not for work. He talked to the big bosses there, asking about investment opportunities.

"Well, he didn't have enough money to invest in shipping, so they suggested farming instead. We had to leave the city for that, though. We hated not having any way to tell you where we'd gone, but we thought you would never leave the Forbidden City again."

"It hurts me how close we were to one another," I say. "The Temple of Grief is just on the other side of Baiyuan Mountain, isn't it?"

"It's not close," Mama says. "But it's not as far away as Peking is. So, yes. If you had left, you could have found us, possibly."

"How could you afford this place?" I ask.

"Oh, it was very cheap. It had been abandoned by some magistrate. The house was crumbling. The fields were overgrown. There were no farmers. But we did a lot of the work ourselves. We repaired the house and worked the fields. Thankfully, the first harvest was very bountiful. We were able to reinvest more money and expand. Then we rented out some of the land to tenant farmers. Your father was able to buy more land to then turn around and rent out again. I had no idea he had such a head for business."

"I'm proud of him," I say. "Of all of you. I was so scared..." I'm almost embarrassed to say what I was afraid of in light of just how well Baba has done.

"I understand," she says. "You didn't know. You couldn't know. All you could do was worry."

"What's next?" I ask. "Will Baba take a concubine and try for a son?"

Mama laughs. "No. He says he's too old for that. And I'm... Well, I'm too worn out. Five daughters is more than enough."

"But what will happen to all this when you are gone?"

Mama shrugs. "Your sisters will all marry well. Mingming is already engaged to a court official."

"A Manchu?" I ask.

"No," Mama says. "A Han. Can you believe it? The new emperor, Emperor Honghui, has made many changes, including appointing Han people to important positions. It has helped temper a lot of unrest among the Chinese."

"Really?" I ask.

"I have to think you had something to do with that," she says.

I shake my head. "Emperor Honghui didn't know I was Han."

"But you still helped him see how important it was that he consider the Han people if he wanted his dynasty to survive. You were a good empress, Daiyu, even if you didn't realize it."

"Then why did you go quiet?" I ask. "I thought you were upset with me."

"No," she says. "No, I was just thinking about Lihua and Mingxia."

"What about them?"

"Daiyu, are you sure Lihua said that Mingxia was dead?"

"Yes. She said that Mingxia's death was why she went to the Forbidden City. Without her mother, she had nothing on the outside."

Mother presses her lips tightly for a moment before speaking. "Mingxia is alive."

"What?" I ask after sitting dumbly for a moment and waiting for Mother's words to sink in.

"We haven't seen Mingxia since the night...since the night she took you from us. But we have...kept tabs on her. She owns a house not far from here. She's very much alive."

"But...then why would Lihua lie? Why would Lihua tell me she was dead?"

"I don't know," Mama says. "That's what worries me."

I try to shrug it off. "But Lihua has what she wants now. She has the emperor's son and I'm gone."

"But you said that Honghui would never make her empress. And several of the other concubines are pregnant. If any of them have a son, he could make that child his heir ahead of Lihua's child."

"What are you saying?" I ask harshly. Honestly, I don't want to think about this right now. I'm home, finally, where I belong. I just want to enjoy this while I can and not worry about Lihua and her horrible mother.

"Lihua wants to be empress," Mama says. "She has already killed two people, including the dowager! She wanted to see you swing from a white scarf. Don't you think she will do whatever it takes to get what she wants?"

I sit back in my chair and fidget with my fingers. If Honghui holds true and refuses to appoint Lihua as his empress, there is only one way that Lihua could become empress—she would have to kill the emperor.

And she would have to do it soon. Before another son is born. If Lihua were to kill Honghui now, while her son is Honghui's only possible heir, then she would be made the dowager empress by default. She would rule all of China in her son's name until he came of age. And even after her son became emperor, she would wield considerable influence over him.

Pain wells up from my stomach to my heart and tears fill my eyes. I'm not exactly sure why I'm crying. Many reasons, I suppose. I'm worried about Honghui first of all. What if he's already dead? No. If that were to happen, the news would travel quickly and the entire country would mourn. I can still save him. But that means going back. It means leaving the family I only just now found.

"I don't want to lose you again," I say.

"Oh, Daiyu," Mama says. "You'll never lose us. Besides, you told Honghui the truth, didn't you? Things will be different this time. And Mingming's husband will be a court official. You will surely be able to see her."

I nod and wipe the tears from my eyes. Yes, things will be different this time. Better.

"But what can I do?" I ask. "I don't have any evidence that Lihua is up to something? I can't even prove that the child is not her son. It's just my word against hers."

"If you want to stop Lihua, you have to be just as ruthless as she is. She would kill you if she could. Can you say the same thing?"

"I'm not going to kill Lihua," I say.

"That's not what I meant," Mama says. "It's *your* life on the line here. Are will willing to do whatever it takes to survive? To save the man you love?"

I let out a long exhale. I don't know what Mama is planning, but whatever it is, I hope I have the courage to follow through.

31

My heart beats thunderously in my chest as I approach the west gate of the Forbidden City. The little vials Mama had given me threaten to weigh me down like an anchor as they sit in the pockets of my sleeves, one in the left sleeve and one in the right. Am I really going to do this? There are so many ways things could go wrong. But if I have any hope of getting rid of Lihua, saving Honghui, and retaking my rightful place as empress, I have to take the chance.

It is twilight, with the sun setting and shadows long. I wear a cape with the hood pulled low to cover part of my face. My hand shakes as I approach a guard and hand him a note along with several large coins.

"This message must be delivered to the eunuch Jinhai at once," I whisper to him. The guard squints and bends forward to try and get a better look at my face. I turn aside and pull my hood closer. "Hurry! The message is urgent!"

The guard hesitates, but I suppose he finally decides that sending a note isn't very risky. It isn't like I am bribing him to let me into the palace.

"Wait here," he says. He then whistles to another guard who is standing on the other side of the door. "I'll be right back."

The other guard nods and moves to the center of the doorway, a better vantage point from which to keep an eye on everything, I suppose.

"Who are you?" the now lone guard asks me.

I take a few steps away and don't answer. The less he knows, the better. Every second that ticks by is agony. Is Jinhai going to come? What if he can't get away? What if he can't sneak me into the palace? What if he's been arrested for the role he played in helping me escape? What if he's dead?

I'm nearly to tears, worrying about all the terrible possibilities, when the gate opens and Jinhai steps out. He looks around eagerly, and when he sees me, we run to each other and embrace like the old friends we are.

"My lady! I've been so worried about you. I'm so glad to know you are safe."

"I'm fine," I tell him. "Hurry, I need to get into the palace. I have a plan."

"Of course," he says. He starts to lead me by the hand, but then he quickly releases me. It wouldn't be proper for a eunuch to be seen touching a woman.

"Step aside for my honored guest," Jinhai tells the guards. The guards glance at each other, but there is nothing they can do to stop us, so they do as they are told.

Once we are inside the great red walls, we have to be even more cautious. The guards would not have been familiar with my face even if they had seen me, but here in the Forbidden City, and especially the inner court, everyone will know who I am. Jinhai leads me to one of the many small palaces that have remained empty since Honghui has so few concubines.

"Why did you come back?" Jinhai asks once we are safely inside and the door is shut. I can't help but shiver. Since the building isn't being used, there is no fire to chase away the chill or bring light to the darkness.

"The emperor, is he all right?" I ask.

"Yes. He's fine. Well, he is clearly despondent. He misses you. I think his sadness is making him ill."

"Ill?" I ask in alarm. "What do you mean?"

"He's been tired lately, weak. And he can hardly keep any food down."

"When did this start?" I ask.

"The day after you left," Jinhai says. "How long have you been gone? Four, five days?"

It took a couple of days for Mother to procure the vial for me, and then another day to travel back to Peking. But it seems as if I did not come back quickly enough. Once I escaped, Lihua must have realized the danger she was in. Her plan to see me swing from the end of a white scarf had failed. She was probably poisoning the emperor little by little. If she did it all at once, there was a greater risk of her being caught since his food could be tested for poison that strong. But if she was only giving him little amounts of poison every day or at every meal, the end result would be the same, but it would be harder to blame Lihua for it.

"Is Liling preparing the emperor's food?" I ask Jinhai. I need to know how she is getting him to ingest the poison.

"No, of course not," Jinhai says. "Do you think Liling would ever step foot into a kitchen?"

"Then, is she fixing his bowl for him?" I know I'm grasping at straws. Honghui knows how dangerous Lihua is, or he at least suspects it. Why would he let her get close enough to him to poison his food?

"I don't think so," Jinhai says, but then he goes quiet, thinking. "She is present for most of his meals. She insists. She says that with you gone, he needs someone watching over him."

I pace the room, thinking. I then remember how she poisoned me. "The tea! Is she preparing his tea?"

Jinhai's eyes go large. "Yes! She usually does prepare his tea for him."

"Don't you see?" I say. "The emperor isn't sick. He's dying. Liling is poisoning him."

Jinhai practically spins on his heels to run to the door. "We must warn him!"

I grab his sleeve. "No! Stop. We must remain calm. It's only a small amount. No one would be able to detect it. If you accuse her of such a crime without evidence, you'll be arrested for treason."

"Then what can we do?" Jinhai asks.

"I have a plan," I say. "But I need to be present when Liling and Honghui are eating. I need to be there when she prepares his tea."

"What are you going to do?" Jinhai asks.

I reach into my right pocket sleeve and hand him one of the vials. "I'm going to drink the poison."

"No!" Jinhai says. He tries to pull away from me, but I hold his arm fast.

"I have to! It's the only way. This is the antidote. As soon as I stop breathing, once I appear dead, pour it into my mouth. But be discreet! I don't want anyone to know you are involved. It should revive me."

"Should?" Jinhai asks with a gulp.

"Well, I've never tried it before. But I have it on good authority that it will work."

"Oh, my lady!" Jinhai whimpers, and for a moment, I feel bad asking all this of him. If anything goes wrong, if I die, he will surely blame himself. But what else can I do? I can't do this alone.

"Snap out of it!" I say, shaking him. "Stop sniveling. I need you!"

He sniffs and wipes his nose with his sleeve before clearing his throat. "Yes. Yes, my lady. I can do this. I'm sorry."

I place my hand on his shoulder to help calm him. "There is no need to apologize. I'm scared too. But I have to do this. Liling has taken everything from me, but she won't be satisfied until she is the empress. And the only way she can do that is by killing Honghui. I can stop her."

"By killing yourself?" he asks, his face gray with fear and worry.

"I won't die," I say. "I know I can count on you."

"You put too much trust in me, my lady," he says, dropping his head and shaking it in shame.

"You put your trust in me first," I say. "You saw potential in me that no one else did. You and Suyin. The only reason I ever became empress was because of you two. You believed in me then. I believe in you now."

His eyes water. "I miss Suyin. I wish she were here now."

"Me too," I say, doing my best not to cry. I need all my strength now to do what has to be done. While thoughts of Suyin make us sad, I think they also give us strength. She wouldn't want me to fail.

"What do you need me to do?" Jinhai asks.

"Sneak me into the room where Honghui and Liling are eating," I say. "I need to be there when she poisons his tea."

"I can try hiding you among the kitchen maids when they serve his food," Jinhai says. "But it might be difficult. You might be recognized."

"Even if I am, the maids should hold their tongues, don't you think? It wouldn't be proper for them to speak in the emperor's presence."

"That's true," he says. He fetches a kitchen maid's uniform, and then he styles my hair simply, leaving it loose around my face to try and hide my features as much as possible.

"It will have to do," he says. I follow him to Emperor Honghui's kitchen, shuffling my feet and keeping my face down. Hardly anyone looks our way. Who really looks closely at a servant? In the kitchen, I watch as dozens of maids line up to take one of a hundred bowls of food to the emperor's dining hall. The maids deliver their bowls and then rush back here to deliver another one. When there are only a few bowls left, I grab one and insert myself in the line. The girl I cut in front of gives me an annoyed look.

"She's new," Jinhai tells her.

The maid nods and goes back to her business of carrying her bowl. Jinhai walks alongside me as we walk from the kitchen across palace grounds to the emperor's palace. My hands are shaking so terribly, I am afraid I will drop the bowl I'm carrying. When we enter the dining hall and I see Honghui, I stop. He looks terrible! I fear he could die at any minute. Why does no one seem worried about him? Where are his doctors?

I forget what I'm supposed to be doing, so Jinhai takes the bowl from me and pushes me aside. Along one wall, several maids have lined up to await any orders from the emperor. If he wants more rice or more of a certain food, the maids are ready and waiting to do his bidding. I shuffle to the end of the row and watch.

Honghui is sitting at the head of the table. Lihua is seated next to him on one side. Yanmei is also there, sitting across from Lihua, so her back is to me. A couple of the other pregnant concubines are present as well. They are all chatting happily, but worry is etched on their faces. I suppose they are attempting to cheer Honghui up, but his health is clearly in a bad place. I only hope it is not too late for him to recover.

Lihua motions toward a maid, who then carries over a tray of tea things.

"The doctor prescribed a new medicine for you," Lihua says as she puts some tea leaves into a pot and then fills it with hot water. "It is sure to make you feel better."

I keep a close eye on her as she prepares the tea. I don't see her slip anything extra into it, but I don't need to. For a moment, I worry that Lihua *isn't* poisoning Honghui. What if he really is just terribly sick?

I can't worry about that now. It doesn't change my plan. As soon as Lihua hands the teacup to Honghui, I step forward.

"Stop!" I yell. Everyone looks at me and gasps. The teacup in Honghui's hand shakes, and I fear he will drop it, ruining everything, but he at least has the soundness of mind to put the cup down on the table.

"Daiyu!" Honghui says and he manages a smile.

"What are you doing here?" Lihua asks.

"I'm here to stop you from poisoning the emperor!" I declare.

There is a new round of gasps from everyone present. Lihua's eyes go large and her mouth gapes for a moment.

"How dare you?" she says. "Guards, arrest her!"

The guards have entered the room, but they don't immediately follow her orders.

"I am still the empress," I say, holding my hand out to the guards. "Something you will never be."

"Be careful, Daiyu," Lihua says through gritted teeth. "You know that I can destroy you."

"Not anymore," I say. "I know that you are poisoning the emperor, and I can prove it."

"What?" Lihua shrieks. "This is preposterous!"

"Your Majesty," I say to Honghui, "give me your cup."

Lihua reaches for the cup herself, but she is too far away, so Honghui snatches it up first. He then holds it out to me, his hand shaking. I take it from him with my left hand and try to sneakily reach into my sleeve with my right hand.

"Everyone saw Liling prepare this tea, did they not?" I ask. Everyone sitting around the table nods their heads and looks to one another for confirmation. I use the moment that no one is looking at me to open the vial and tip its contents into the cup before hiding the vial in my sleeve again. It only takes a second, but it feels much longer to me. I think that I must have been seen, but no one says a word. Lihua looks at me, her nostrils flaring.

"To your long life, Liling," I say, holding the teacup out to her. Her eyes narrow, but I see a smirk on her mouth. She knows that whatever she put in the cup will not be strong enough to hurt me from only one drink. She thinks that nothing is going to happen and that I am the one who will look the fool. I only hope I retain consciousness long enough to see the look on her face.

I drink the poisoned tea.

It tastes terrible! I grimace and flick my tongue in and out in an attempt to rid it of the acrid, dirty taste.

Lihua humphs and crosses her arms. "See? Nothing. Arrest her!"

At that, my whole body seizes. My vision goes black and my brain feels like it is on fire. I'm on the ground, shaking, and I can feel foam or drool coming out of my mouth. Everyone screams. I can't see what is happening, I can't react, but I can hear everything.

"Daiyu!" Honghui is over me, shaking me.

"No! No!" Lihua screams. "It wasn't me!"

I hear more screaming and crying. My throat closes and I can't breathe.

"Daiyu! Daiyu!" Honghui is crying now. But I don't hear Jinhai. Where is he? What if he can't reach me? I then realize that in the panic, the guards are probably holding everyone back. There is a stabbing pain in my chest and my lungs feel as though they are going to burst.

I'm dying.

32

"Daiyu."

I can't open my eyes, yet I can see...something. The world is fuzzy and gray. There is a light, and someone comes toward me.

"Daiyu."

"No..." I mutter and my eyes water.

The light gets brighter, closer. No, not the light. A woman. A woman is the light. She's dressed all in white and the light is coming from her. I can feel her sit next to me and her face comes into focus as she strokes my cheek. It's Empress Caihong.

"No," I say again even though I'm sobbing. "I don't want to die."

Caihong laughs, her voice high and clear. "Then it's a good thing you didn't."

"What?" I gasp and open my eyes.

"Daiyu!" Strong arms hold me so tightly, I can't see who it is. "Thank the gods you are awake."

I cough and pull back, drinking in the fresh air like a

drowning person, which I guess I was. Honghui lays me back on my pillow.

"I saw...I saw her..." My voice is raw and it hurts to talk. Another figure brings me a cup of water. Yanmei. She holds the water to my lips and I drink it eagerly.

"Who did you see?" Honghui asks.

"Caihong," I say. "She...she came to me. I thought I was dead."

"I thought you were too," Honghui says. "But Jinhai managed to bring you back."

"Jinhai..." I look around and see him standing nearby, his hands to his mouth and tears in his eyes. I reach out to him and he comes to my side, gripping my hand.

"My lady," he sobs. "I thought I'd failed you."

"No," I say. "You did everything just right." I glance around again as my vision clears. "Where is Li...Liling?"

"I had her arrested," Honghui says. "I can't believe you drank poison for me. How did you know that she was poisoning me?"

"I know her. I knew she would do whatever it took to become the empress."

"I thought she was the source of my illness," Honghui says. "But I couldn't prove it. I kept letting her serve me, trying to catch her in the act. But I never saw her put anything in the tea. Did you see her?"

"Yes," I say flatly. What's one more lie, especially one that will save the life of the emperor? Now, his health can recover and she can be locked away. She can finally be held accountable for the dowager empress's death and for poisoning the emperor.

"But why did the poison nearly kill you when it hadn't yet killed the emperor?" Jinhai asks. I shoot him an annoyed look. I'd only filled him in on half of my plan. The other half of my plan, the part about poisoning myself and letting Lihua take the blame is something I plan to take to my grave...hopefully many years from now.

It was something I had to do. Lihua was willing to kill me to get what she wanted. I had to be willing to kill myself to stop her.

"Maybe because you are smaller than me," Honghui decides. "She was putting in enough poison for a grown man, not a little woman."

I smile and nod my head. "That must be it. Where...where is she?"

"The Cold Palace," Honghui says. There is an anger in his voice. "I should have her put to death instead of letting her have the gift of killing herself."

After everything Lihua has put me through, the idea of her dying makes me sick.

"Can I speak to you alone?" I ask Honghui. He nods to the others, who all bow their way out of the room and close the door.

"What is it?" he asks me.

"Can you spare her life?" I ask him.

"What?" he asks. "She almost killed the empress of China! She has to pay."

"And she will," I say. "Remaining a prisoner for the rest of her life will be punishment enough, I'm sure."

"If she lives, she will always be a threat to you."

"Maybe," I say. "But I just can't do it. She and I, we are more similar than either of us would like to admit. Killing her would be like killing part of myself."

"Fine," Honghui says, but he is clearly not happy about it. "I suppose I could exile her far away, under constant guard. I'll send her somewhere that she can never trouble us again."

"Her and her mother," I say. "She said her mother died, but that's not the truth. And her mother is even more cunning. She's dangerous. I have a feeling they concocted their plan together. Telling me that Mingxia was dead must have been a way for Lihua to try and reassure me her reasons for being here were pure."

"I'll have her arrested immediately, then. To hell with both of them."

I reach up and touch the side of his face. "Do not be angry. We are together now. That's all that matters."

He reaches up and puts his hand atop mine, then he kisses my palm. "What about the boy. My...Liling's son?"

I shake my head. "You know he's not your son."

"I know. I believe you. But he's not Liling's either. I don't trust she will be a good mother to him now, but I don't expect you to raise him. He can't be my heir. He needs to be sent away."

"Maybe my father can adopt him," I say. "He has no sons of his own. I'm sure he and my mother would gladly accept him as my little brother. He's just an innocent babe in all this."

"Your...your father? I thought he... Well, I guess I don't know anything about you."

I sat up in the bed. "What would you like to know?"

"Everything."

I open my mouth and pour out my heart to him. I trust him completely and know that my future is secure. No longer in disguise. Not in hiding. And finally, no longer in danger.

I am the empress, and I'm here to stay.

The End

ABOUT ZOEY GONG

ZOEY GONG was born and raised in rural Hunan Province, China. She has been studying English and working as a translator since she was sixteen years old. Now in her early twenties, Zoey loves traveling and eating noodles for every meal. She lives in Shenzhen with her cat, Jello, and dreams of one day disappointing her parents by being a Leftover Woman (剩女). Learn more at ZoeyGong.com.

facebook.com/ZoeyGongAuthor

goodreads.com/zoeygong

bookbub.com/authors/zoey-gong

ABOUT AMANDA ROBERTS

 Amanda Roberts is a USA Today bestselling author who has been living in China since 2010. She has an MA in English from the University of Central Missouri and has been published in magazines, newspapers, and anthologies around the world. Amanda can be found all over the Internet, but her home is AmandaRobertsWrites.com.

facebook.com/AmandaRobertsWrites

instagram.com/amandarobertswrites

goodreads.com/Amanda_Roberts

bookbub.com/authors/amanda-roberts-2bfe99dd-ea16-4614-a696-84116326dcd1

ABOUT THE PUBLISHER

RED EMPRESS PUBLISHING

Visit Our Website To See All Of Our Diverse Books
http://www.redempresspublishing.com

Quality trade paperbacks, downloads, audio books, and books in foreign languages in genres such as historical, romance, mystery, and fantasy.